THE DSA SEASON ONE, BOOK FIVE

DARK
IMPULSES

Also by Lou Paduano

The Greystone Saga

Signs of Portents
Tales from Portents
The Medusa Coin
Pathways in the Dark
A Circle of Shadows

Greystone-in-Training

Hammer and Anvil

The DSA

Season One
The Clearing
Promethean
The Bridge
Spectral Advocate

THE DSA SEASON ONE, BOOK FIVE

DARK IMPULSES

Lou Paduano

Eleven Ten Publishing LLC

GRAND ISLAND, NEW YORK

Eleven Ten Publishing LLC
282 Fareway Lane
Grand Island, NY 14072

Publisher's note: This is a work of fiction. Names, characters, places, and incidents either are the product of the author's imagination or are used fictitiously. Any resemblance to actual events, locales, or persons, living or dead, is entirely coincidental.

Printed in the United States of America
Edited by JD Book Services.
Cover art design by MiblArt

First edition published 2020

Library of Congress Cataloguing in Publication Data
Paduano, Lou
Dark Impulses / Lou Paduano

LCCN: 2020900277
ISBN-13: 978-1-944965-26-6 (paperback)
ISBN-13: 978-1-944965-25-9 (eBook)

For Nonna and Nonno,
who always offer their love and support.

CHAPTER ONE

The dripping sound woke her. The small pitter-patter falling along the soaked carpet at her feet sent wave after wave of dizzying echoes into her unconscious thoughts until she was snapped awake. Her first thought landed on the sink: a poorly maintained bathroom basin in a two-star motel on a dead-end road. Of course it was the sink. It wasn't until Morgan Dunleavy licked her lips that she realized it wasn't water running from the sink, but blood dripping down her face.

"Where?" she asked to the shadows of the room. The small stream ran from the top of her head, down her nose, and over her lips. She spat as the question left her, which interrupted the steady dripping.

From behind her, light split the dark beige curtains of the motel room. The bed lay upended along the far wall. It matched the state of the rest of the furniture in the cramped space. Morgan fought to breathe, the blood trickling into her mouth and over her tongue. Her eyes struggled to adjust to the moonlight which faded behind the fast moving clouds in the winter sky.

"Zac?" she called out. Her head pounded. Everything hurt. Everything screamed to be noticed and mended. She searched for her medical kit. Her mother had given it to her after Morgan graduated. She always carried it with her. The small bag rested out of sight; it was lost in the darkness, just like everything else.

"No," a voice growled in response. Two small pebbles of light flickered from the far side of the room. A tapping returned to the background, this time that of a heavy-soled sneaker — red and white with blue laces. Morgan's eyes widened. They attempted to refocus despite the swelling along her temples. "Your boy toy isn't here, Morgan."

Her mind snapped to attention, and the cloud over her thoughts was gone the second his words cracked the darkness. She reached to wipe away the blood and remove the matted strands of dark hair from her face. Her hands refused to obey her. She pulled again, and the force caused her to cry out. Tied hands strained against the chair beneath her.

"Oh, hell."

The tapping ended and the figure in the shadows stood. His chair flew across the room. It joined the table, the nightstand, and the bed in a crumpled heap. His eyes remained wide lights, and deep red ran along the edges of his pupils. His jaw was clenched, which kept his voice throaty and guttural. She recognized him anyway by the gun in his hand—the same Ruger he always carried.

"Ben," she muttered as her partner stepped into view.

"You betrayed me!" Ben Riley's empty hand rubbed at his neck. The other shook with fury, yet his sidearm remained locked on his captive. Morgan tried to lift her hands, to talk to her partner calmly and casually. Zip ties clacked against the wooden frame of the chair. She recalled the struggle from earlier. She remembered the argument that started it, and the blood that followed.

Her blood. She bit back the panic creeping into her chest. "This isn't..." Ben shook his head as soon as she opened her mouth. She spoke louder. "Ben. You need to listen to me."

"To your lies?" Spit flew across the air between them. "After what you've done to me?"

"I haven't—"

The gun silenced her, now only inches in front of her face. "You stole my life," Ben cried. His eyes were a deep, dark red that matched his flushed cheeks. Goosebumps ran up his arms, and both were shaking, matching his uncontrolled anger. "You and Metcalf and the rest. You took everything from me! Do you know how that feels? Of course you don't."

He was wrong. She understood what it was like to lose a life you worked so hard to create. The DSA was built for people like them. A second and final chance.

"Ben," she whispered. "Please..."

The gun cocked loudly. Cold eyes answered her plea. "But

you will, Morgan. You will."

The flare of the muzzle was the last thing Morgan saw. Then the world went dark.

CHAPTER TWO
Three Days Earlier

"Here's something new."

The DSA briefing room buzzed with personnel. Analysts lined the wall, careful to avoid the swinging door as more shuffled inside. The chairs at the cherry table were occupied, all eyes on the hovering DSA logo projected on the screen in the middle. Ben picked at the paperclip on his briefing summary. Morgan dug into the details while flipping across reports and vital statistics. She had grown into the lead agent role nicely. Zac hovered in front of his chair in the soft glow of the deep blues and golds of the logo.

Metcalf soaked in the atmosphere. This was the DSA, the bustle of an impending operation. Every piece of the department was working as one to close cases and save lives. The feeling had been missed by the director.

Yet not everything was the same. Analysts filled Lincoln's and Ruth's chairs. Their absence had diminished the effectiveness of the unit, though no one wanted to discuss it further. They focused on Zac instead, as his flair for the dramatic always hid his nerves when delivering a case.

"Zac," she said. The sharpness of her tone caused the Head of Operational Support and Research to wince. His irritation with her was well known, and the number of eyes shifting to the floor surprised no one.

Many in the room shared his discomfort. Only Morgan appeared unfazed by the rising tension. She had recently sided with Metcalf in an attempt to bring Lincoln in quietly for questioning over the deaths of two Army Intelligence officers. The mission had failed, but it had solidified their bond in some ways.

No, the problem lay elsewhere. With Ben, in particular. The relative newcomer refused to look in her direction. Their snippets of conversation over the past week had barely constituted a full sentence in total. Their shared silence had stemmed from his discovery of the Grissom File: an unflattering look at the death of his predecessor and Metcalf's former deputy.

The operation had taken the man's life, though disagreements existed over the true cause. Few believed Metcalf had made the right call, and the after-action reports reflected their disapproval. She had allowed Grissom to die, left him behind for the safety of the team. It was the right call in her eyes, despite the protests of others. She had tried to inform Ben of her view, attempted to stymie his growing resentment and anger. It wasn't easy.

Not with another player whispering in his ear. Greg Sullivan's presence was hardly expected, yet had been consistent of late. He held no seat at the table. Rather, he circled the arena while scanning the crowd with smiles and camaraderie—something Metcalf dismissed as below her station. It was a mistake, and one Sullivan capitalized on in front of her.

He was a damn vulture picking at the refuse of the DSA's divided loyalties, driving further wedges between her people when she needed them the most. It had to end, and it all started with Ben. If only she could make him see that.

Her momentary thoughts returned to the waiting Zac, who nodded silently. He clicked ahead. The lights dimmed and the logo faded.

"Right," he said. Local reports filtered on the screen. They spread across the wall-length display in the back of the room. "Four arrests within the last two weeks. Four murderers."

"Doesn't sound so new," Morgan said. A smile grew along her lips.

"Well... I... That is..." Zac stammered.

"Sounds like a closed case," Ben said.

Zac took a breath and shook his head. "I'm building up to it. Call it dramatic tension."

"Didn't know your fan fiction had finally been published," Ben replied.

"Very funny," Zac said. "But when the Blade versus Buffy

crossover finally happens, you'll be calling me a forward thinker."

"No, I will definitely be calling you something else."

"Gentlemen," Metcalf said with a roll of her eyes.

"HA!" Morgan said with a snort, awkward in the silence of the room.

"Agent Dunleavy?"

The lanky black woman shrugged. "Sorry. That was the first funny thing I've heard today."

Metcalf shook her head. "Get us to the point, Zac."

"I was." Groans echoed in the room. Everyone joined in, from Ben to the analysts along the wall. Zac waved his hands in the air, trying to get everyone's attention. "Hey, I was!"

Sullivan grinned as he lapped the space. He said nothing, but his looming continued to distract Metcalf from the briefing. His presence wasn't required; it never was, according to their division of labor. He handled the politics of the department, while Metcalf handled the day-to-day operations. It was a clear line, and he crossed it — continued to cross it more with each passing day.

When she returned to the shifting screen, Zac was already moving ahead. "Anyway, this was kicked over to us for standard analysis when local authorities reached out for an assist. It isn't the victims or the arrests that dinged the weird-o-meter — patent pending. It's the murderers themselves. Random citizens acting out their bucket-list murder scenarios."

The display shifted. The first file opened to reveal a man in his mid-forties and balding. Deep, recessed brown eyes and a small goatee offered little in the way of character for the man.

"Our first one here is Anthony Ritchie," Zac continued.

Ben stirred, head snapped to attention. "Why does that name sound familiar?"

"Cause I just said it, Riley. Keep up." Another click, and Zac's presentation continued. Ritchie's face shifted to the corner of the wall display. In its place, crime scene photos from a bank filled the wall-to-wall projection. "Ritchie, bank teller for over twenty years, stabbed a client with a letter opener for trying to sneak Canadian coins in with his US deposit."

"Sounds extreme," Ben muttered.

"Did I mention he stabbed the woman thirty-three times?"

Morgan closed her briefing packet. Her nails tapped lightly along the top. "Maybe more than extreme."

"Maybe." Zac grinned to the woman, but his expression immediately faded when Metcalf signaled for him to proceed. The images changed once more. Another face—this one of a woman restrained by officers in her home. Tattered wallpaper lined her dining room. Crime scene photos ran alongside the depicted arrest. A man sat in his recliner, hunched over the arm rest with a chunk missing from the back of his head. "Crystal Moore bashed her husband's skull in while he was watching the six-o-clock news."

"Infidelity?" Metcalf asked.

"N-no… no…" Zac stammered. His cheeks darkened and he let out a long breath. "Not even close, actually. According to the officer on record, the husband's only sin was that he failed to put his dishes in the sink."

"I hate that," Ben scoffed.

Morgan's eyes thinned as she snapped a finger at her partner. "Knock it off."

Ben waved his hands in surrender and Zac cleared his throat. "Like I said, two more of a similar type occurred the previous week. Donald Puff ran down his paperboy with his truck for being late. Agnes Welmont smothered her husband for snoring too loud."

The images filled the display, then split to four respective columns. Crime scenes photos lay atop the victims and their killers. The four murders left the room silent in contemplation.

Ben spoke up first. "Influx of mental patients to the area?"

Zac shook his head. "No history of mental illness for any of them."

"Drug users?" Morgan said. "Prescription or otherwise?"

"Not from the reports," Zac answered. "Other than blood-pressure meds for Mrs. Welmont. No priors either. Neighbors described each of them as one of those nice and quiet types until bam."

"Bam?"

Zac's shoulders lifted then fell before he collapsed into his waiting chair. The projector dimmed, and the lights returned to the room. Sullivan's pacing ceased as he took position next to the wall—always watching, always waiting. Metcalf wanted to scream at the man, but she held her tongue as more questions flew across the table.

"Where are we talking about?" Ben was first. He was almost always first, mostly because the man lacked the ability to keep quiet.

"What?"

"You never said where this was happening?" Ben said, a hand to his bloodstained tie.

"I didn't?"

"No…"

Zac rubbed his chin thoughtfully. "I could have sworn I did."

Ben's jaw tightened. "Are we doing shtick now?"

Zac hesitated, then turned to Metcalf. "Director?"

Metcalf set down her glasses. "Buffalo, Agent Riley."

"New York?" he asked.

"That would be the one."

Ben stood. "When do we leave?"

All eyes lowered, and all muttering ceased. Silence took hold, the unspoken concerns ripping through each and every member of the department. Everyone knew Ben's story: where he had come from, and its importance to him. His exposure in Buffalo would also shed light on their agency, and could risk their work both past and future.

Metcalf held the man's question for a long moment. She was slow to stand, delicate fingers pressed hard along the cherry tabletop. She leaned forward, never blinking, never retreating from the man's query. He needed an answer. They all did. More than that, though, they needed to have the talk that had been put off for far too long. Metcalf tilted her head for the door.

"A moment of your time, if you please, Agent Riley?"

CHAPTER THREE

Zac stared at the coffee machine. Steam rose from the full cup of bubbling black ooze. Liquid dripped from the corner of his mug. The remnants of his over-sized mug sloshed around like a whirlpool. He eyed the sugar packets and the jar of powdered creamer, contemplating how much would help him at this point of the day.

Briefings always took their toll on him. They always took hours of prep work. Then there were the questions from the field team to anticipate. Once they understood what the top priority was for the day his work shifted immediately to handing out tasks, building teams within the support staff, and setting up hourly updates to keep Metcalf and Sullivan apprised of any developments. All rested on him. But that wasn't why he stared blankly at the thick black sludge no one could mistake for coffee in his mug.

He did it because of the woman by his side.

"That wasn't awkward," Morgan breathed, her lips inches from his ear. Her every word sent shivers down his spine.

Small cliques formed throughout the room. They waited impatiently while Metcalf and Riley had it out in the hallway. Everyone had sensed the conversation coming, though the Buffalo situation had brought it to a head a week sooner than the best predictions in the office pool. Typically, Zac spent these awkward moments alone working through routine assignments, or tracking incoming progress reports from the overnight staffers.

Having Morgan by his side, having her breath wash over him, made him forget the business casual attire draped over her muscular frame and remember her shadow dancing along her bedroom wall. Her perfume filled his senses, fragrant and intoxicating. He moved the coffee cup closer to his lips to drown the aroma as he sidled away from her.

"Not at all," he said in a low tone.

"I'm glad it gives us a minute," she continued. She reached across him for a stir stick. Her hand grazed his, before she snatched the thin plastic between her fingers. Her smile caught the periphery of his vision, inviting him for a closer inspection. Instead, he turned toward the rest of the room and the dozen unsuspecting staffers not bothering to glance their way. Morgan followed suit. She leaned against the folding table behind them, and sipped at the steamy Styrofoam cup of coffee in her hand. "You've been avoiding me."

"Morgan."

Her brown eyes drilled him for answers. "We haven't talked all week. You also haven't been over since that night."

"I've been working," he said, his voice barely a whisper over the mutterings of those around them.

"Come on, Zac."

The lie was weak, but it was all he had to offer. He *was* avoiding her, avoiding everyone outside of work. After his shift, which extended later and later with each passing night, Zac found himself driving his rust-covered Chevy through the streets of Bethesda for hours. There was nowhere for him to turn, no one to speak to about the thoughts plaguing him. Before Morgan, he had always turned to his wife for support and a sounding board. Though he could never go into details about the work he did at the DSA, Claire's voice always brought him comfort. Now when she spoke all he imagined was her heart breaking at his betrayal.

He had betrayed Claire with the beautiful woman that sent his heart racing with a single touch and drowned him in ecstasy with only a word spoken. Morgan supplied Zac with a confidence he had never known in all his years with his wife. She inspired him with nothing but a smile. She wanted him on a level no one else ever had. He never wanted to lose that feeling. Yet there was Claire to consider. Always Claire.

Morgan reached for Zac's shoulder, and he shifted farther away. "I have been working, Morgan. And please, let's announce to the room we slept together."

"Whoa," Morgan replied. Her face sunk. "What's wrong?"

Zac bit his lip. "It's nothing. I'm just tired."

"I can tell," she said with soft words. Her hand rubbed his back and he let her fingertips knead into the mounting tension buried beneath his skin.

"Morgan," he said, though his voice was distant. It was a weak appeal for her to stop. His eyes closed at her touch. "Please."

She smiled, inching closer. Those around them continued to gab without care. "I'm trying to help," she whispered. "I'm a *very* good helper."

"I know." His eyes snapped open. Then, he took her hand and let it fall away. Holding tight to his mug, he stood in front of her. "I know you are. That's just not what I need right now."

"Oh," she said with a nod. "Of course."

Zac peered around the room, surprised at the lack of stares—at least on one level. On another, he was not surprised at all. Even though he had hired most of them to fill positions on the research floor—with Metcalf's approval of course—he still remained completely isolated from them. Invisible—like he had always been.

Except with Morgan.

"You'll be heading out with Riley?" he asked. He kept the conversation focused on work as much as possible. Both glanced across the room while Metcalf and the agent from Buffalo continued their less-than-cordial discussion.

Morgan shrugged. "If Metcalf gives him the green light. There's no one else around for field work."

She took a long sip to cut off a follow-up question. Her eyes flitted to the cup and then the ground. Zac understood the statement on multiple levels. Abigail Winslow, their latest recruit, had been found dead in her apartment the day after she signed on to the job. Then there was Lincoln MacKenzie to consider.

Zac still didn't understand the circumstances behind Lincoln's absence. Only one truth remained about the situation pertaining to their wayward colleague: Morgan was holding secrets back from him. She was well aware of what happened in Des Moines, an incident he had discovered but was asked to bury by the ever-commanding Director of the DSA. What truly happened at the Savery Hotel remained hidden from him.

He believed Morgan was different. That she trusted him, that it was more than a physical attraction. Both served the DSA, he thought, yet with each passing day the silence between them on the subject gnawed at him; the divide grew thanks to Deputy Director Sullivan's knowledge of the incident.

Finally the question broke to the surface. "No word from Lincoln?"

Deep brown eyes widened, then cooled. "None," she said. "I wish I knew what happened."

Zac's hands tightened on the mug. He bit the inside of his lip, but he refused to press. Lincoln was in the wind because of her actions and those of Metcalf. The pair had conspired to help Lincoln despite his complicity in two murders in Des Moines. Zac had heard the audio, thanks to Sullivan's growing surveillance operation.

Where was Morgan's loyalty? To a killer like Lincoln? To the DSA? Or to Zac, the man she appeared to pursue at every turn? Was that the truth, or was she using him, seducing him with her body, toying with his desire just so she could further manipulate the situation? Did she actually care about him at all?

His doubts surged, begging to be released in a scream. He buried them with the growing questions, and was thankful when Morgan pointed to the bright display of the current operation on the back wall.

"Any clue what this could be?"

"None," Zac said. "Local medical examiner came back with overwhelmed adrenal gland. A big burst of adrenaline triggered the rage, then the collapse."

Morgan looked puzzled. "Collapse? You said they were arrested."

Zac's hand shot to his forehead, which nearly spilled the remnants of his beverage. He attempted to rub away the exhaustion and massaged the outside of his bloodshot eyes. The long hours were starting to affect him more than he wanted to admit, especially when it came to briefing the team on items they needed to hear.

"They were." He recalled the lost details he had failed to mention. "Once they were in holding, though, they simply collapsed. Some even in transit."

"How severe?" Morgan asked, staring at the screen.

"As severe as it gets," Zac muttered. "I can't believe I... I..."

"Zac."

He should have included it in the briefing. All four killers, the nice and quiet people living their small lives, had died from whatever had caused their uncontrollable rage. He should have mentioned it, instead of thinking about the woman in front of him. The woman with the soft eyes comforting him, excusing his mistake with a simple smile. It was one he fell for every time, when every shred of evidence told him to run away and reclaim the life he'd avoided for the last week.

Zac turned away, sullen and much more alone than he had been all morning. "Be careful, Morgan."

"Always."

He refused to look back, wishing *he* had been careful. He should have known better than to sleep with Morgan, known better than to fall for her so completely. But that was the thing, wasn't it? Zac didn't have a single clue what he wanted anymore.

CHAPTER FOUR

Ben watched with great interest from outside the briefing room. Through the myriad staffers he caught them side by side. He watched them exchange small touches and slight grins. Morgan and Zac failed to note any witnesses to their discussion, but he saw them. He saw them *very* well.

"Ben?" Metcalf asked as she snapped her fingers in front of his face. He'd heard her every word, every sigh and huff of breath that left her lungs, everything she cared to share with her subordinate as well as what remained unsaid. When they'd stepped into the hallway he waited for the fireworks to start, waited for the yelling to begin. She had started small, calm words used to bring him to the table, but she had held back what she really wanted to say. "Agent Riley?"

"Hmmmm?"

Metcalf recoiled, hands clasping her hips. "Thanks for joining the conversation."

"Is that what this is?" Ben had grown tired of the dance. Nine days had passed since his meeting at Fort Meade. Days of walking on eggshells around each other, casual greetings traded in the hopes of learning the intentions of the other without actually engaging. Things had remained civil between them despite the constant weight of his meeting with Sullivan and the Assistant Director of the NSA, Donald Stallworth.

Both refused to let the noise, the politics, get in the way of the work. It had stewed in their silence, however, and festered like a cancer. The unspoken questions needed addressing, but they remained among the untouchable subjects of religion and political affiliations.

Ben was fine with the delay. Any chance to avoid a discussion on the subject gave him more time to figure out a way to understand what had been occurring behind the scenes of the DSA. He needed more time to choose his position. On one side was Sullivan's veiled threats under the promise of freedom. On the other was Metcalf's lies of omission when it came to his recruitment and the loss of the previous agent in his shoes, Jacob Grissom. Neither was the ideal selection, yet they were the only cards on the table.

"Excuse me?" Metcalf balked.

"Just say you don't want me on this case." Ben leaned against the wall across from the briefing room, catching the glares of a group of support team staffers exiting for the stairs. He smiled at each as they passed.

Metcalf cut off his view. Her cold glare swallowed his smug grin. "I don't want you on this case."

"There, don't you feel better?" Ben pushed off the wall and moved for the room. "Can I go now?"

"Ben," she said, her hand wrapped tight around his arm. "I've had enough of this. We should talk about what happened."

He waited until the hand fell away. "You mean what your pals Sullivan and Stallworth said about you? Or are you ready to talk about Agent Grissom?"

Metcalf sucked in a deep breath, then fell silent. Since Ben's arrival the subject of Grissom had come up in whispers and innuendo. From the moment Ruth Heller mentioned his name, Ben tried to learn all he could. No one talked about what happened to him. No one wanted to make eye contact when the subject came up. Grissom was dead and buried, but his shadow loomed over them all.

Sullivan had let the cat out of the bag in what he hoped would be an enlistment opportunity to his side of the fence. Ben never cared to learn what Sullivan's agenda truly was, but the threat of fulfilling his legal obligation to the State of New York and the jail sentence awaiting him made it clear the deputy director was not going to let Ben simply walk away from the decision. What Ben had managed to pull away from the file handed over by Sullivan was that Grissom was all but sentenced to death by Metcalf when all reports to the contrary explained he could have been saved.

"Listen to me, Ben," Metcalf started, her words strained.

He shook his head. "I think I've heard enough, Director. I'm here. I'm doing the work."

"There's more to it than that," she replied. Annoyance crept into her voice, though she did her best to bury it behind her considered words.

"There always is, isn't there, Director?" He held the title out, emphasizing it like the hissing of a snake's forked tongue.

"Cut the passive-aggressive crap," she snapped, finger poised at him. "I've put up with it for too long. You want to do this here and now?"

Staring eyes grew in number from the briefing room. Ben shifted deeper along the corridor to get out of view. "No," he said. "I don't care to hear anything from you, Director. Not the lies, nor the half-truths you feel like spinning today."

"That is—"

"If you don't want me to find out why people are turning into killers at the flip of a switch, then that's your call."

Metcalf fell silent. They were both aware of the current scorecard when it came to operatives in the field. Lincoln was MIA, though Ben had yet to learn the reason behind his absence. Winslow was dead. Zac had limited experience and not of the good variety, unless the situation in Buffalo needed another potential hostage-slash-victim in the mix. Ben was her only choice in the matter.

"You work the case," Metcalf relented. "You go where Morgan goes. At all times."

"I don't need a chaperone in my hometown."

"Yes you damn well do," she said. "You get recognized and it is over, Ben. You know that, don't you?"

Another threat of jail time. It was starting to become a pattern. Ben shrugged. "You just said it, so it must be true."

Metcalf winced. "This is about saving lives and the case at hand—not what happened to you. Personal issues cannot take priority."

Ben started down the hall. "I'll pack my bag, Director."

Metcalf called after him, "I have your word on this?"

Ben ran his fingers along his bloodstained tie. His face went cold. "Of course. Don't you trust me?"

CHAPTER FIVE

Ben grabbed his overnight bag from the open locker. He lowered the duffel to the nearest bench to peek inside. The prerequisite clothes, ID, cash, and accessories sat within the confines of the small black bag. His spare sidearm was nestled in a side pocket as well as a paperback novel he only read on the road. Something light with a few jokes tossed in to keep him in good spirits. Just the way he liked things.

Satisfied the bag was set for travel, Ben slammed the locker shut. He paused with his head resting against the cool metal. His conversation with Metcalf had gone as well as could be expected. Little hope of reconciliation remained—both harbored far too many secrets; both were unwilling to take the first step to bridge that singular divide between loyalty and trust.

"Dammit," he muttered. He punched the locker, the jab setting him back a step. He should have pushed for answers, demanded the truth behind so many open questions that troubled his every thought. Metcalf had monitored him, surveilled his work and his life for years. Why? For what possible reason had Ben been chosen for this position? Had he been groomed for the role through her machinations?

Those were the selfish thoughts plaguing him. The more pertinent information he required involved his predecessor, Grissom. He had died during a field operation much like their current assignment. The situation had been littered with unknowns, and they had been unprepared for the possible outcomes. Grissom had met a gruesome end, abandoned by the director. Everyone else believed he could have been saved. Either it had been planned on her part, clearing the way for Ben's arrival, or she had merely wanted Grissom out of the way to maintain her control on the department. Those were the only two options imaginable after a week of rumination, yet the pit in his stomach held out for a third path.

Frustrated, Ben clicked the lock back in place and spun the dial, not that a covert agency like the DSA couldn't access his locker at any time they wanted. He grabbed the bag and slung it over his shoulder, his bloodstained tie whipping along his chest. A figure blocking the door stymied the hurried agent's departure.

"Agent Riley," Deputy Director Sullivan called. The man pushing his late fifties was wearing his traditional sweater vest and khaki combination, though he appeared to be sweating beneath the ensemble. Sullivan's eyes were black holes under the panel lighting running along the ceiling, and the bags underneath sagged to his cheeks. He closed the door behind him.

"Sullivan."

"I'll ignore the bile that comes with my name."

"Don't," Ben replied. "I try very hard to make it sound as bad as you look right now. Sleepless nights?"

Sullivan ignored the comment, attempting to hide the apparent weariness, the unkempt beard bristling along his chin, and the thickening stress lines running the length of his forehead with a grin. "Whatever your feelings, helping the Council helps the DSA. That is, if you *are* helping us?"

So much for a social visit. Sullivan was all business as usual. He had pressured the agent since their meeting at Fort Meade under the auspices of a friendly assessment. Sullivan had demanded information about Metcalf's agenda. Though he had offered up evidence of her surveillance of Ben's life and the Grissom File to steer Ben to an easier decision, he had finished with a threat of jail time. Sullivan required ammunition to use against the woman, most likely through the Inter-Agency Council in control of the department's overall status. Rather than air out their grievances they had decided to draw up sides, pulling and manipulating everyone they could in the effort. Ben was one such lucky soul caught square in the center of their power struggle.

"I've done what I can," Ben said, refusing to glance at the looming Sullivan. "Passed along everything I could. Conversations. Files. Reports."

They were stalling tactics, and both recognized them—even behind the bluster of Ben's words. Sullivan tilted his head. "Surface details. I—we need more. Are there any ongoing operations off the books? A project kept secret even at the highest levels?"

He was on a fishing expedition, trying to gauge Ben's reaction to the open-ended questions. Sullivan's need was apparent. Was it pressure from the Council? From Stallworth? What did they need on Metcalf to force her out?

Sullivan's hard glare softened and a hand reached for Ben's shoulder. "I'm offering you a way back, Ben. Your life, the way it should have been."

That was the carrot of their arrangement. Compromising Metcalf provided a way for Ben to reclaim his former life. Where Metcalf attempted to keep him from his home at any cost, Sullivan handed him his freedom for a pittance of betrayal and disloyalty.

"We'll talk when I get back," Ben said, shoulders slumped. Sullivan's grin broadened, and the door to the locker room unlocked once more.

His daily bruising completed, Ben snapped the zipper of his overnight bag closed and stood. Sullivan waited at the exit. Shadows from the lighting attempted to hide the exhaustion in his eyes. He was getting desperate, his latest push much harder than before. The time for stalling was at an end.

"Make the right choice, Ben. The future is counting on you."

CHAPTER SIX

Damn the luck.

Sullivan cursed to himself, hand pressed tight to the wall outside the locker room. *The gall of the man.* Riley stalled for time without a care to his fate. Easier methods existed to test one's loyalty. If Sullivan were given the choice, Riley would receive the bitter end of the stick — and a one-way ticket to prison.

The beleaguered deputy director cared little for Riley other than what his answer could provide. He was merely another pawn in the plan. That was what took the majority of his days now, the subtle manipulations maneuvering the pieces into place so he could achieve his goals. Objectives fell within reach at last, after months of soul-searching and years of swallowed dreams.

An operation, in Buffalo of all places, was the last thing he needed. His last foray in the city had nearly cost him everything when his impatience had gotten the better of him. Now, the universe conspired against him to destroy his efforts.

If Riley stood at his side there would not be an issue. They could simply oust Metcalf from her chair and see about the business of bringing the DSA to the forefront of the intelligence community. The DSA could burst into the light to help the masses. That was the mission and should have been for everyone.

Instead, Riley's loyalty — and the critical information locked in his Neanderthal-like skull — remained with Metcalf. Not so much in his words, but in the man's eyes. Those damnable brown orbs twisted Sullivan's every word; they peered through him as if seeing the truth behind each claim. It was impossible, but Riley's actions made it clear winning over the departing agent was not in the cards.

Other tactics were necessary to protect Sullivan's secrets. Months ago he'd made a play he regretted, a search that had cost him an operative and almost his entire future. If Riley learned the truth of his involvement, if questions were asked of the right people, it would expose his current agenda. His life would be in jeopardy, his last chance shattered.

"Dammit," he muttered. Sullivan pushed from the wall and paced down the corridor in solitude. Staffers nodded in his direction and he replied with a warm smile. Distancing himself was not the smart play. That road was what had led to Metcalf's predicament. He was too wise to fall into the trap of power — even power as elusive as the head of the DSA.

Instead, he allowed his stature to fill the halls. He attended each and every meeting available. He memorized the names of those surrounding him and invited them to share their days with him. Lord, how it disgusted him. So much time wasted, all for what came next.

Now it was all at risk because of a series of murders in the so-called *City of Good Neighbors*.

Sullivan skirted through the thinning crowds and rounded the corner to the shooting range. Ever since Lincoln's disappearance the room had barely been used. Rare was the analyst that carried a permit let alone a firearm. The lock clicked behind him to secure the room from unwanted company.

Intervention was required. Yet any action taken also came with a risk. Should Riley stumble on any foul play during his stay in his hometown, he might turn to Metcalf completely. Not a loss, per se, but a less-than-desirable outcome.

The risk was negligible compared to the Trust learning the truth through their incessant need to question everything. There was no stopping Sullivan now, and the frustrated bureaucrat confirmed that notion with only a phone call.

It rang twice before clicking over. The voice on the other end of the line filled the speaker with gravel and spite. A smile grew on Sullivan's face at the anger booming in his ear, all without a single word spoken.

"I have another job for you," Sullivan commanded when the rage fell away to silence. "I think you'll enjoy this one. It involves an old friend of yours."

CHAPTER SEVEN

There was only one question on Morgan's mind by the time she entered the South Park Avenue precinct. *Why the hell do people still live in Buffalo?* She was freezing. More than freezing, in fact. Her chills had chills. The newspaper touted the second straight week of subzero wind-chill as if it was a major victory instead of an event indicating the future ice age that threatened to consume the region.

Towers of snow obstructed the first floors of homes lining the streets. Every turn of their car sent waves of panic through her. Oncoming traffic remained unseen until the last second, forcing her to clutch tight to the wheel the entire trip.

"They actually celebrate getting this much snow?" Morgan asked her partner upon arrival. No answer was given, not that she needed one. Only lunatics glorified not being able to enjoy the open air for six months out of the year. Lunatics and Alaskans. The silence from Ben unnerved her, however. His focus was solely on the sights and sounds of the city he still called home.

His resentment was palpable. The indignity of having to hide among his peers was a torture. He wasn't any better by the time they entered the station. Tucking his head to his chest, Ben let a wide-brimmed ball cap and a pair of sunglasses obscure his presence. When she asked him to wait in the lobby, an argument fomented yet never escaped his lips. His jaw clenched and his teeth gnashed, but only a nod answered her request.

Morgan handed the desk sergeant her badge, the DSA logo drawing more questions than the man with the New England Patriots cap. Before calls could be made to confirm her identity, their local contact appeared.

Detective Eric Baxter stood at a modest five and a half feet tall. His thick neck strained to gaze up as he approached the waiting agent. Thick black nose hairs flapped in the breeze with each release of breath, mixing in nicely with his mustache. His hair was combed over, a desperate attempt to keep the dream alive, but one that worked with his overall appearance. A small bump over his belt completed the picture.

He offered a hand to usher her into the precinct. Baxter shared a quick glance with Ben, who paced solemnly in the background. Morgan fought a smile at her partner's silence while wishing she didn't enjoy the quiet as much as she did.

"Glad to have you here," Baxter said. The pair traveled briskly through the precinct in a straight line to his office. A chair awaited her, and she took her place in front of his desk while he made the slow circle to the opposite side. Framed images of the *Three Stooges* decorated the walls. Statues of rosy-cheeked patrolmen swinging over-sized batons stood on every available shelf and along the entire front edge of the detective's desk.

"Really?"

Baxter laughed, deep and guttural. "Is it really that much of a surprise?"

"Well, I've heard of inter-agency cooperation in theory," she joked.

"Say no more," Baxter said. He slapped the end of his desk with thick sausage fingers. His laughter continued as he slid as close as possible to the stacks of paperwork littering the metal tabletop. "Most of the time I see it from both sides, but on something like this? Let's just say I had started restocking the fallout shelter in case the sky started bleeding."

"That bad?" Morgan said, wondering if blood would have been a welcome change of pace from the snow.

Baxter grumbled. "I've never seen as many whackadoos killing each other like there literally was no tomorrow."

Morgan shifted uncomfortably in her chair. "Yet there's nothing to connect them."

"Not a thing. And we're at six now," Baxter replied, hands on a large smattering of files on his desk. He caught the questioning stare on Morgan's face and nodded. "Yeah. Two more last night. Just finished the reports on them—not that I have much to fill out when it comes to these things."

"Were they domestics like the others?"

"No. These were places of employment," Baxter corrected. "Horrible bosses, and I'm not talking the movie. Still, there's no connections other than the random rage then collapse. Different professions, lifestyles, places of residence, gender, ages, everything."

Morgan was used to that. There was a reason the DSA was called in on cases like this. The agency's experience with less-than-normal circumstances, including the reason behind the rash of deaths, made them more suited to take the lead. Baxter's openness toward cooperation eased the process, unlike most cases. Still, it would have been nice to have a more easygoing operation, especially with the cold wearing her down mere hours after their arrival.

"And they were all unable to answer questions?"

"Being dead can do that to a person," Baxter muttered. His gaze shifted away from the office toward the lobby and the silent player in their drama. Ben continued to pace around, head low, though Morgan noticed a distant look in his sullen eyes. He wasn't in the present at all; she knew he was surrounded with mementos of the past at every turn. She had been hoping this wouldn't happen. That Ben would still be able to do the work even with the constant threat of being recognized. His sarcastic nature, while irritating and grating on all levels, had proven useful in coercing information.

Morgan pulled Baxter back, obscuring his view. "All of them?"

Baxter fell back in the seat. "Half in transit to lockup. It's like they were hardwired for the kill, then fried a circuit."

Morgan nodded. Behavioral changes of this magnitude were rare. Environmental situation aside, little could change a percentage of the population as much as what was going on in Buffalo. Six people, random citizens without a criminal record between them, suddenly becoming so angry with the world as to lash out at the person next to them — sometimes the person that had been by their side for decades — and commit murder? Nothing natural caused that. Only one option remained viable, and not one she enjoyed thinking about.

External factors were involved. *Someone.* Someone had done

that to those people. It had to be. She only had to figure out the who and the how.

"What did the M.E. come back with?" Morgan asked. Baxter's eyes wandered to her partner down the hall. Morgan waved the detective back once more. "Don't mind him. Off day."

Baxter chuckled. "Hate 'em. Three cups of joe, triple sugar, and you can't pry the smile off."

Morgan struggled to laugh with the jovial detective. When he fell silent, she waited a long moment before reiterating the question. "Detective?"

"Hmmm? Yes?"

"The medical examiner's report?"

"Right. Yes. I have it." Baxter dug through the paperwork on his desk. File folders toppled to the floor to clear a path to a bright green folder at the bottom of the pile. He held it up triumphantly before passing it across the desk to the waiting hand of the patient DSA agent. "There you go."

Morgan flipped through the preliminaries. The M.E. had provided constant updates for Baxter as more test results came in. Elevated adrenal levels were noted in every autopsy; their cause remained unknown. Something hid in their blood—an undetermined anomaly. "Some kind of drug?"

"That's the current thought here. No idea how or why at this point, but—"

"Nothing specific on the drug itself either."

"Right," Baxter agreed, rubbing his mustache in long strokes.

"Whatever it is seems targeted on the adrenal gland," Morgan said as she paged through the reports. "It sends our killer on their rampage, then when the adrenaline high ends their system just shuts down."

"Kaput."

"Who would do that to a person?" Morgan snapped the file shut. She pushed the report back toward Baxter, who caught it firmly under his fingers to keep it from joining the rest of the paperwork on the floor of the cramped office. "Someone did this to them, making them victims of circumstance, not the killers they appeared to be. But why? Why make their last act on earth so incredibly violent?"

"Like I said before. Glad to have you here."

There had to be a connection, something just out of view

from everyone. Even with the local department on hand for the last two weeks it left a lot of ground to cover, but now with six incidents recorded it provided them enough of a starting point to find the missing link in the evidence chain. They had something to go off while also working with the medical examiner to find the specifics of the drug being used to create homegrown killers. Then they could use that information to figure out a way to counteract it.

"I—" Morgan stopped herself, acknowledging her absent partner in the lobby. "We need to know everything about the people affected. Home address. Place of employment. Friends. Relatives. Everything. We'll also need a copy of the M.E.'s findings. We can stop by their office tomorrow morning for a more thorough examination, but I like to be prepared."

Baxter stood. "Cause you can prepare for something like this?" The overweight detective's cheeks blushed at her silence. "I'll get right on it."

"I'll wait," Morgan said, remaining in the uncomfortable chair.

Baxter pored over the pile of paperwork needing to be duplicated for them. His smile refused to disappear, though it faded slightly at the sight of the mountain of copying ahead. "Right."

His back popped and his knees creaked as he lifted the files. Morgan mouthed a word of thanks before he left the office for the copier down the hall. She shifted against the cold metal of the chair, a chill rushing through her multiple layers of clothes as if she were still outside in the January wind.

She glanced back to the lobby and her pacing partner. Morgan worried about the wayward stare, the quiet anger seeping from his movements. He clearly wasn't thinking about the case. She required his insight and banter, though she loathed to admit it. They worked well together and needed to now more than ever. There had been six murders so far. Whatever ate at him, whatever memories plagued his troubled thoughts, he needed to work through them and fast.

Before that number climbed any higher.

CHAPTER EIGHT

Ben hated waiting. He was never good at it, and patience had never been a virtue in his vocabulary. Even at a young age he had struggled with waiting. There was the time in third grade when he'd had to use the restroom only to find the stalls and urinals occupied. Instead of biding his time, Ben had rushed into the girl's room next door. He still remembered the scream from Gillian Lane alerting every teacher in the corridor.

It didn't stop him from finishing his business before being escorted to the principal's office.

Pacing the lobby of the precinct house reminded him too much of those circumstances. Only, in this case, discovery meant a one-way ticket to Attica instead of detention.

Ben lowered his Patriots hat and continued his steady lap through the confined space. Morgan sat impatiently down the hall in Detective Baxter's office. The curls of her hair ran over the back of the chair. There were too many people in the precinct coming and going. It took all his nerve to keep his mouth shut when a greeting slipped his way. He offered only a nod of his hat as a reply.

His silence was necessary. The act of admitting that, though, caused bitterness to rise in his throat. Metcalf wasn't wrong, and he needed to prove himself capable of following a simple directive. Her trust mattered, though his intentions were not noble. Winning Metcalf over served a purpose.

Either Metcalf was telling the truth and was looking out for his best interests, or she lied through her teeth and her trust would lead to his betrayal. Metcalf or Sullivan—the choice constantly pulled at him.

He tired of the internal argument. He tired of the endless pause. Hell, he tired of pretty much everything. Fed up with pacing, Ben slipped into the building. He could just as easily remain silent in the corner of Baxter's office, where the threat of recognition was minimal. He wasn't in his precinct—wasn't where he had spent years of his life serving and protecting his hometown.

That was what surprised him the most when he saw the name. It sucked the breath from his lungs, a gut punch at the sight of the small sign on the nearby desk. There was a placard carrying the name he spent weeks searching for, and it caused him to forgo caution and deviate from his partner for the open floor of the precinct.

WRIGHT

Emily Wright? Could finding her have been so simple? Had she merely changed precincts in his absence? He had never considered the option, never thought such a change possible. But why hadn't he? He surrounded himself with the abnormal, the strange and weird. Maybe he was the one who had changed and the world just continued as it always had.

Optimism carried him across the floor toward the desk. The name drew him in like a tractor beam. As he reached for the nameplate, a tall kid in uniform rounded the corner and grabbed for the chair. He carried a smile and a fresh cup of still-steaming coffee.

He paused before sitting, a curious look at the stranger in the Patriots hat. "Can I help you with something?"

"This your desk?" Ben asked, almost growling to disguise his voice.

The kid nodded. "Derek Wright. And you are?"

Ben shook his head, tucked his hat lower, and backtracked for the open corridor. "In the wrong place. Sorry to bother you."

He spun on his heels and turned down the hall before resting against the wall. *Stupid. Damn stupid.*

The name had almost slipped from his lips. The circumstances of Emily's disappearance had almost betrayed him due to his growing concern. It mattered more than keeping his secret, mattered more than maintaining the lie about his exile from his home. She was his last connection to this place, and she was missing.

Ben closed his eyes and banged his head lightly against the plaster. Horace Waters would know. The detective held connections with everyone in the city. It was the reason he had found it so easy to frame Ben the way he did, to set up Ben's public fall from grace and have no one bat an eye at the improbability of such an occurrence. Waters had gone into hiding after that though, leaving nothing but questions in his wake.

If only Ben could find him, use what information he had to track down Waters and obtain the answers he needed—including the location of Emily Wright. Instead, Ben took a deep breath and swallowed his fleeting hope. That wasn't the mission and never would be. His life in Buffalo was over. It was time to accept that.

CHAPTER NINE

Morgan found him in the hall, alone and lost in thought. Her hand on his shoulder shook him back to the present.

"What's going on?"

He kept his head low toward the floor. He used the sunglasses to block the curious glares that were growing in number, but also to hide from her. Ben had been supposed to wait in the lobby. Hell, if she had her way, he would have waited at the motel room until after the meeting was done.

The risk to him was too great, but he wouldn't hear of it. Being home had that effect. It seemed to give him a need beyond personal security, just for the chance to see familiar sights.

Morgan tucked the stack of paperwork securely under her arm as she sidled closer to her partner. Eyes bored into her back. Baxter waited for more: a word of thanks, appreciation at the expense of hundreds of pages of documents or maybe for the loss of his time for the effort. Either way, all she offered was a nod and a slight wave. Ben followed suit with a tip of his cap. The pair made it to the lobby before she asked again.

"What happened back there?"

"Nothing. It's fine," Ben replied. He opened the door, and the wind threatened to dislodge the files from her grasp. Morgan huddled close until she reached the outside world. Ben hurried behind her. His hat obscured the approach of a gathering group of officers in front of the motor pool. "That everything?"

Morgan ignored the question. She quietly cursed the weather. The howling wind and the sleet were determined to send her sliding to the cold concrete. Winter might have been the natural state in New York, welcomed with open arms by some, but those people were absolute maniacs. She hated the cold. The chill ran down to her bones. Her multiple layers of clothes failed to offer her even the slightest reprieve.

"Morgan?"

"Huh?" She shook her head, then smiled. "Did you say something? I have trouble hearing when you growl."

"Are you serious?" he asked. The pair rounded the corner for their rental. The foot traffic lightened thanks to the late morning hour. "I'm trying to —"

"Practice your Batman impression?" she said. "I figured. Not a fan."

Ben sighed. "Is that everything on the case?"

Her grin widened at his tired, careful words. His frustration mounted, especially since he was unable to work as he typically did in the field, thanks to the risk involved. It made for a peaceful day in her opinion.

"There's enough to get us started," she said. She tapped the files lightly, careful not to lose any as a surge of wind slammed across the lane. "Lots of ground to cover. I'm meeting Baxter at the medical examiner's in the morning to go through the autopsy reports."

"Think Baxter is on the level?"

"Other than wanting to deck you for that hat?" She flicked the brim of his cap, then started for the car at the corner. Ben stayed close, hands buried in his pockets. "Were you *trying* to draw attention?"

"Yes," Ben admitted. "To the hat. I almost wore a Dallas Stars jersey too. Now back to my question."

The rental clicked and the trunk opened. Morgan dumped the files inside her waiting bag. "You're so suspicious when you can't engage."

Her laughter caused him to wince. "Please stop."

She wrapped her arm around his shoulder and pulled him close. "Personally, I like the strong, silent you."

"Really?" Cold breath escaped in a puff from his lips. The passenger-side door opened, and she ushered him in. "Cause I hate him."

Morgan leaned close. "I know. That's the best part."

CHAPTER TEN

The walls closed in on Lincoln MacKenzie. It had been over a week since he went on the run. During that time he attempted to hide in plain sight while he figured out his next move. It had left the man haggard and in search of comfort. His travels had led him to the Walkway Diner just outside Bethesda. What it had really led him to, however, was another mistake in a growing list of them.

Even at the late hour plenty of patrons occupied the place. Most were solo affairs, regulars sharing a location and nothing else. They grumbled greetings and offered their muted responses to the day's events. They spoke about everything from the weather to politics. Whenever the conversation ran longer than a sentence or three, though, the awkwardness returned and silence took hold.

Lincoln preferred the quiet. Truthfully, he preferred the burger-and-fries combo on his plate, both drowning in ketchup. A meal out was an extravagance. Most of his time had been spent holed up, weighing options and seeing little in the way of ones that failed to include a trip to prison and lethal injection.

He'd screwed up. Two men had died by his hand. His blood was on site, enough DNA to close the case even without a high-priced attorney. There was no denying the charges. He had killed them to protect the man he had been sent to end: the Witness.

Of all the players in their little drama, the enigmatic figure with the opaque lenses held all the cards. All the answers were his to dole out. Lincoln needed those answers, needed to understand the secrets being kept from him. The DSA had changed during his tenure. Their priorities had shifted, hidden agendas had grown, and secrets were taking over in place of transparency. The danger also grew, building with each operation in an unending string of threats.

What were they fighting for anymore? Who were they protecting? The country or the department? Was he working for a singular entity, or were other agendas hidden in the shadows playing them for puppets?

The Witness dangled those answers before Lincoln. The famished agent had held off on reaching out for the last week, ever since failing to win over Morgan to his cause. He had tried to explain his thinking, attempted to show her his sincerity at doing the right thing, but the Witness' involvement clouded everything. It had driven her away and with her his last chance at finding a way back.

He was alone, cut off from all friends and colleagues. It left him with only enemies on all sides — including the patrons of the small diner.

His unease in the public place started with a brief glimpse from the waitress behind the counter. From there, it slowly shifted to more staring and the nudge of another employee. Shared whispers interfered with his eating, so Lincoln placed the burger back in the basket. Venturing out had been a mistake. Most of his meals had arrived sealed in plastic sleeves, freeze-dried and stored for emergencies in a storage unit kept under his dead brother's name.

He had merely wanted a damn burger. A simple-enough excuse for the trip — one that now cost him.

He was made. Through the opening to the kitchen, Lincoln caught sight of one of the cooks on the phone. Nervous glances in his direction made it clear the man was talking about him.

Sirens completed the picture for the silent patron. Grabbing a handful of fries and jamming them into his mouth, Lincoln inched to the edge of his booth. He reached back and snatched the burger, wrapped it in a napkin, and tucked it in his pocket. Ketchup ran in thick globs down his lips and along his fingers. He flicked them at a passing waitress, who screamed. Grinning, Lincoln raced for the rear of the place, the flashing lights showering the diners as he entered the kitchen.

The cook pulled a knife at his arrival. The brave soul with

sweat soaking his brow stayed close to the sizzling patties at his back. Lincoln raised his hands, hugging the far wall for the exit.

"We know who you are," the cook said. He crept closer with the knife. Lincoln stopped and his eyes flitted for the dining area. The flashing lights were stationary. The sound of fevered steps and closing doors filled the air. The knife slashed the space between them, calling for Lincoln's attention. "I can't let you leave."

"You don't want to do this," Lincoln grumbled.

"We don't appreciate killers, mister."

"Neither do I," Lincoln replied. The cook brought the knife down in a wide arc, overreaching from his position. Lincoln caught him at the wrist and snapped the flimsy joint in a quick motion. The clatter of the knife on the ground was lost to the man's cries. He fell to the ground, clutching the limp appendage. Lincoln crouched close. "If I was truly the monster you imagine, what do you think would happen next?"

"You… You maniac!"

The door crashed open. Uniformed officers spread out to secure the dining area. Guns drawn, they rushed for Lincoln's position.

The surrounded agent stood over the cowering cook. "They'll get you fixed up, pal. Don't be a hero next time and just serve the damn burger."

Cold air blasted Lincoln. The shouting of officers in the kitchen was muted by the wind sweeping the alley. Cops converged from the north and forced the fleeing agent to the shadows of the opposite direction. At the southern tip the alley collapsed in a heap of refuse and fences, save for a narrow breezeway barely able to fit a single runner.

Exactly as Lincoln had planned it.

No matter his intentions in the restaurant, preparation remained critical to Lincoln's every move. The diner had been selected for its location, for the breezeway impossible to block, and for its proximity to his haven.

The cacophony of sirens and shouting faded in the three-block blitz to his safe house. The location stood in the form of a derelict apartment building. Row housing occupied the left side of the street and the single structure made up the right. Shattered windows, graffiti brickwork, and seeping water issues condemned the property. It had been a clear sign for Lincoln to use it as he saw fit.

Lights flashed behind him. He leaped from the chain-link fence surrounding the structure to avoid being seen. Diving beneath the light and through the tall, overgrown brush, Lincoln edged deeper into the shadow of the building. The police slowed to shine a spotlight through every cracked entrance and shattered pane. He waited in the brush for them to pass before ducking inside.

Three floors up and down to the end of the hall, Lincoln found his supplies: mostly weapons and ammunition. They were his tools for the coming struggle. Lincoln inched for the window, occasional lights shining in his direction. He crept along the side of the frame, then collapsed. The vantage overlooked the entire block all the way back to the diner. It not only offered him a glimpse of the front entrance, but the distance to his hideaway also gave him ample time to prepare to escape through the multiple points developed during his stay.

No one followed his movements, so he allowed a breath. Settling along the rotted floorboards, Lincoln removed the burger from his pocket. The bun had torn away from his escape, but the patty remained intact. He shoveled the remnants into his mouth, bliss escaping in a low moan.

It had been so much trouble over a simple meal. Des Moines was still trailing him and he couldn't outrun that forever. Morgan should have understood. He was doing this for her, for Ruth, and for the DSA. Loyal to the end, no matter what anyone else believed.

A passing neighbor caught his thoughtful shadow in the window. She said nothing and made no motion for her phone. The code of the neighborhood went that far, at least. But how long could he count on that? She would eventually see a wanted poster, consider the possibilities of a reward, and then where would her so-called code be?

Every choice, every hour he waited, put him at risk. There was only one option left to him.

Lincoln removed the index card, which had been at his side ever since he'd found it in the wreckage of the Savery Hotel. The secrets held in the scrawling along the back teased only a taste of the answers awaiting him. Now it was time for the rest of the puzzle. Now it was time for the Witness to keep his promise.

Lincoln dialed the number listed on the front of the card and waited until the line clicked over.

"It's me," Lincoln said. "I'm ready to have that chat."

CHAPTER ELEVEN

The sun was long set, and the moon had become an inconsistent visitor behind a layer of thick graying clouds. More snow was in the forecast. January in Buffalo? Snow was *always* in the damn forecast. Hours of scouting possible connections between the six homegrown killers had left a pit in Morgan's stomach and an aggravating twitch under her right eye.

"We could have split the area," Ben whined.

She stopped in front of a place called Sidelines, one of a dozen bars littering the area and one central to the majority of the murderer-slash-victims' place of either residence or employment. The two of them had asked dozens upon dozens of questions up and down the block. Some to ditzy waiters, some to experienced managers, and all to no avail. At the end of their seventh hour canvassing their fourth strip of businesses, Ben's incessant complaining gave her a twitch on top of her current twitch.

"Could have," Morgan said without looking. She didn't need to see the pouting face under the obnoxious Patriots cap. *At least he ditched the sunglasses.* She peered into Sidelines' front window, noticing the light crowd and relative quiet. It appeared peaceful compared to the themed college-aged bars of the last block and the retirement kingdoms of the one before that. Her heels ached, and her shoulders were knotted from the long day. She was ready for a break.

"Look, Riley," she started, inching closer to the building to avoid a group of diners heading for the bar. She lowered her voice, hoping Ben's name wasn't recognized by the group. A breath escaped her when the group entered without a glance in their direction. "I don't like it either, but if word gets around that the poster boy for everything wrong with law enforcement is wandering the streets, all of a sudden we have a bigger problem than we need."

"People forget," Ben said. He shoved his hands into his pockets for warmth.

"Have you?" she asked. His head bowed. "I rest my case."

Ben huffed. "All right. But I call dibs on food here. I'll get cranky if I don't get some wings in my system."

Morgan's stomach rumbled in agreement. She reached for the door. "How do you know they serve wings here?" Ben replied with a slight smirk. "Ah, right. Buffalo."

"Chicken wings and Scott Norwood. Buffalo."

Morgan ushered Ben into the warm air of the bar with a gentle push. "Want people to remember McKinley was shot here instead?"

"If I said yes, would that make me a bad person?"

"Yes."

He shrugged. "Oh well."

Morgan stopped him from heading farther into the dining area. "Questions first. Then food."

"Lead on," Ben replied with a bow.

Morgan did so, escorting them to the far corner of the small bar and grill. She took the bench seat facing the crowd, which gave Ben a clear view of the wall and little else. Grumbles escaped him, but they dissipated when a waitress trailed their arrival.

"Getcha some drinks?" she offered, her voice just as perky as her more noticeable assets.

"If you can spare us a minute of your time," Morgan said.

The smile fell from the young woman's face. "Not that kinda place, lady."

"Wow," Ben exclaimed, suddenly sitting at attention.

"Shut it," Morgan snapped at her grinning partner. She placed her badge on the table. "It's agent. Not lady."

"Oh," the waitress said. No more perkiness. No more awkwardness. Just concern remained at what she had stepped into by racing over to the table instead of letting someone else come over. "Maybe the manager should—"

"Probably a good idea."

The waitress disappeared as quickly as she had arrived, refusing to peer back in their direction. Morgan settled along the seat. She was happy to give her feet the rest they deserved, but less than enthused at the widening smirk Ben struggled to hide behind the menu he pulled from the end of the table.

"Not a word," she said with a raised finger.

"I..."

Morgan leaned close. "I'm serious. Keep your eyes on your menu."

Ben casually viewed the list of entrées within the laminate menu. "She seemed nice, is all." Morgan's foot lashed out, catching his ankle soundly. "Ow!"

As Ben reached to soothe his wounded appendage, the manager arrived. He was younger than expected, short, and thin as a rail. His thick strands of black hair were tightly cropped above his ears.

"How can I...?" The man whose name tag read Mr. Manfredi stopped short at the sight of Ben. "Do I know you from somewhere?"

Ben raised his menu to cover his mouth and nose. He shuffled closer to the wall. "Uh..."

Morgan snapped her fingers to pull Manfredi back to her. "No. We're not local."

"I could swear..." Manfredi ran a hand along his chin.

Morgan shifted closer, then slapped at her badge. "We're wondering if you've seen any of these individuals in the last few weeks." The file slipped out of her bag. Her hand reached within, pulling loose the same set of photos she had displayed to more than thirty other businesses over the course of the day. The curious manager focused on each image that came into view.

"What's this about?"

"Have you seen them?" He didn't need any information other than what she cared to share. Unfortunately, they had little to offer, despite their efforts.

Manfredi pointed to two of the photos on the bottom row: the two most recent killers. "I've definitely seen these two. I think they work around here, so they're here pretty regularly. Lunches. Dinners to go. Happy-hour stuff. These others? I can check with the staff."

"It gets busy here?" Morgan inquired, shuffling the photos

into a single stack before handing them to the man.

"Peaks and valleys," Manfredi said with a shrug. "Probably pick up in the next hour or so once the college crowd makes it our way. Lot of competition in the area, but we do all right. Is there—?"

"If you could ask your staff it would be greatly appreciated," Morgan said. "The sooner the better."

"Of... of course," Manfredi stammered, waving the images before him. "Whatever I can do."

Morgan smiled. "Maybe a couple waters?"

"And a double order of wings," Ben said, the menu continuing to cover his features. "Hot. And fries. Definitely fries."

"Oh?" Manfredi paused as confusion spread across his face. "Oh! Yeah. Sure thing. I'll put those in for you now."

"Thank you."

They didn't wait long for the wings. For all its foibles, the city had certainly developed its niche in the food industry. Morgan could not remember a time a meal had tasted as satisfying.

While the two agents ate, they reviewed the work behind them as well as what lay ahead. Manfredi came back with little in the way of information, which matched the other businesses in the area. There was no way to recognize every patron that came into an establishment. Sightings were all they had to work with. There were no discernible patterns. No smoking gun led them to the killer in their midst, one capable of creating others at a whim.

That left them with more canvassing. Going forward, however, it would no longer be limited to random eateries and businesses in a close proximity to the targets. From there on out the victims would become the focus. Family. Relatives. Places of employment. The list grew and grew with possibilities. The weary agents would need help for the next step. Baxter and his team were the obvious choice. Morgan was reticent about it, though, considering the risk put on Ben should he be recognized. What they needed was a better understanding of what was happening around them and the threat involved. The how and the why of it, as Baxter stated.

"I don't see any progress here," Ben groaned. They both stared at the stack of reports amid their empty dishes. Three wings swam in hot sauce between them, begging to be eaten.

Morgan kept her gaze on the files, her stomach bloated from the meal.

"Me neither," she said. "This is the same as the other bars in the area. Enough traffic to connect to a few, but on the same dates as the murders? God knows what Baxter was able to pull in the meantime."

Ben fell back in the seat. "So we call it a night after this and start fresh?"

"Best option I've heard all day."

Ben lifted the plate. "Finish them off?"

Morgan shook her head. "No way. I don't think I have an inch of space left."

Ben turned toward the rest of the dining area. He scanned for a waitress, someone to help clear the table and deliver the check, but then stopped midway. His attention immediately locked on the television screen above the bar, and the plate threatened to slip from suddenly shaking fingers. Morgan moved to help him, and was surprised when he jumped to his feet.

"Ben?"

"Can you...?" he choked out. He rushed for the bar. Morgan trailed his steps, concerned. Ben pushed through the small crowd, pointing to the television. "Can you turn that up?"

"What?" the perky waitress asked over the muttering of the masses.

"The television," Ben said. "Turn it up."

"Ben?" Morgan pulled at his shoulder without success. News broke on the screen as the waitress cranked the volume. "What is it?"

Ben refused to acknowledge her. The newscaster read through his script. The image of a man filled the backdrop.

"...where he was found hanging in his motel room," the newscaster said. "Again, Detective Horace Waters has been found dead. The detective, reportedly missing for some time now, had recently made a splash in the news discovering police corruption and murder tied to local officer, Benjamin—"

A hand grabbed the remote from the waitress and flipped the broadcast back to SportsCenter. Ben remained fixed in place.

Horace Waters. Morgan recognized the name. Everyone at the DSA knew the story that came with it. Horace had ruined Ben's life. He had taken the man at her side away from his city.

Morgan's hand tightened on her partner's arm. "We need to sit down. Now."

Ben nodded, still unable to move. His voice trembled. His hands shook.

"He's dead, Morgan," he said in little more than a whisper. "Just like that. After everything he did to me. Every problem he caused. He's dead."

CHAPTER TWELVE

How? How is this possible? The questions screamed in Ben's mind as he stood in the center of the bar. More heads turned in his direction, drawn by the mutterings under his breath and his glassy stare at a newscast no longer airing on the screen.

"He's dead," Ben repeated. A hand pulled at him, forcing him around. Morgan's grip squeezed as she tried to rip him from his musings. Her eyes probed for a response.

"We need to sit down. Now." It clicked with him at last. Ben started back to the booth in the darkened corner of the dining area. Morgan remained behind. She tossed a reassuring smile to the staring patrons who refused to return to their drinks. "Cousins. Distant cousins."

She was right to a degree. The connection certainly ran deep enough; it was like a limb had been lost and he just found out about it. The dead man was a crucial chapter of Ben's life story. There was Ben before Horace and Ben after Horace. Like a parent kicking a child out of their home when they turned eighteen, that was the effect the man had on his life. Unwanted and unwarranted, he had left Ben with nothing but questions.

Horace was dead, though, and now those questions would never be answered. Suicide on the same day Ben had returned to the city for a case. Was such a feat of circumstance possible? Could anyone truly believe it to be coincidental?

Morgan joined him at the booth and slid into the bench across from him. He kept his head low and near his knees, leaning along the edge of the seat and lost in thought. Her hand reached for him once more, calling out to him. "Ben," she whispered. "I need you to say something. Please."

What was there *to* say? What could possibly sum up the storm brewing in his chest after learning the man who had taken everything from him had gone one step further and ended his own life? He had taken that selfish step, giving Ben nothing in return. No answers. No reasons behind why Ben had been framed or what secret he had accidentally unearthed thanks to his visit to the strange home on Wex Avenue.

Was he happy with the news? Saddened at the man's passing? The idea of this moment, the notion of Horace's death, had never entered Ben's mind before. The very concept was foreign to him, just as the emotions raging through his every thought. Horace Waters was dead. Not by his hand. Was *that* what made him unsure? Angry, even? The lack of closure? He had lost his chance at so many answers that might have given the events of the last year meaning.

They were taken from him. The same day Ben returned to the city.

"He's dead, Morgan."

"I know," she said. "We'll look into it. When we can."

When we can. It was code for 'when it became convenient to everyone else's schedule.' When it mattered to everyone else, or when he became too much of a pain in the ass to ignore. In other words? Never.

"Do you even listen to yourself?" he asked, fingers clenched tight to his knees.

"Ben..."

His eyes burned at her. "He's been missing since the trial. Months, he's been gone—vanished like a damn ghost. We happen to be in town less than a day, and now he's dead."

"It was a suicide," Morgan scoffed. She pointed at the television screen over the bar. "You don't know any of the—"

"You're right," Ben snapped. Curious glances flew toward him, and he shuffled deeper into the booth and lowered his voice, though his anger continued to swell. "I don't know any of it. He ruined my life, Morgan! He took it away from me and I never found out why. And now? How can you not understand?"

Morgan shook her head. "Jumping to conclusions is a waste of time."

"Is that what I'm doing?" His cheeks flushed. He couldn't believe her. Morgan was tossing his suspicions away with such ease. She didn't care. "Because I think I understand the stakes we've been playing and know the score pretty damn well."

Morgan fell silent, reading his expression. At the realization of where his accusation fell, her hand slapped the table. "Come on! You're not—"

"Not what? Not right? Not reading the signs correctly?"

"The DSA would never be involved in something like this. We—"

Ben closed his eyes, falling back against the booth. "Sell me another one, Morgan. Next you'll try telling me you're not sleeping with Modine. How do you see that ending for you, Morgan? Or for him? He's married, for Christ's sake."

Her hands slammed against the tabletop between them. The sound echoed through the dining room, silencing conversations throughout including their own. Morgan stood abruptly, grabbed her coat, and vacated the booth. The bag containing their files slipped over her shoulder. Rushed fingers struggled to remove some cash from her pocket. She tossed the bills to the table without looking.

"Morgan… I didn't mean…" Ben said. The sight of the hurt across her face made him instantly regret his words. She leaned over him, a tall shadow plunging him in darkness.

"Get this crap out of your system," Morgan said through gritted teeth. "And make it quick."

She moved for the door, even as Ben called out to her. "Listen, I…"

Morgan didn't stop. She didn't turn. The door to the bar slammed closed behind her, and the chill of the winter stole the heat from the room for a long moment.

Ben's hands ran the length of his face. He knocked his hat off and tugged at his matted brown hair in disgust. His back sank into the bench. He needed to go after her. He needed to apologize and put it behind them so they could focus on the case. Horace Waters be damned, no matter the questions hanging over the affair. No matter the rage billowing below the surface with every mention of the man's name. That was the best course of action, yet he remained glued to his seat, hands covering his face.

"What an ass," he muttered.

"Rough night?" a voice asked from behind him. Startled, Ben

shifted to greet the deep voice of the man.

"You could..." Before he made the half circle turn the figure closed the distance. Instant heat passed through Ben, and something punctured the back of his neck. Thin, cool metal slipped in and out of skin.

A needle.

"What the—?" Ben never finished the question. His mind screamed from whatever worked its way through him. It moved quickly, and the heat from his neck traveled the length of his body, sending small spasms down his arms and legs. Ben's vision blurred and the man with the thin needle took the seat once occupied by his departed partner.

"I apologize, Agent," the man said, his frame a wave of light in the room spinning before Ben's eyes. "It doesn't get any better for you, I'm afraid. But at least you'll have some fun before the end. We both will."

"You? But you're..." Ben's eyes widened. He realized who the voice belonged to immediately. Stars danced from the periphery, multiplying as the fire burned in his veins. The tabletop closed in and his head collapsed on the surface. The world turned black. Words fell from his lips before the darkness enveloped him.

"You're dead."

CHAPTER THIRTEEN

The pounding on the door shook her from what little sleep Morgan had managed over the course of the night. Streams of diluted sunlight filtered through the cracks in the frayed blinds over the window. Movement came slowly to the groggy agent. She imagined the rhythmic beating to be nothing more than a pulsating headache.

Her feet touched the thin carpet, then shot back to the blankets of the bed to escape the initial cold shock. Morgan grabbed at a pair of socks and slipped them on. As she stood, more knocking ensued on the metal door.

"I heard you the first time," she grumbled. Her head was pounding, and the lack of sleep didn't help. After leaving the bar she had wandered the streets for hours. She hated the cold. She hated the wind. She hated pretty much everything around her, but most of it had been drowned out by Ben's words.

She had held her anger in check when she left. She had stomped along the icy sidewalks, until she'd no longer known where she was. She regretted having to call the cab, but the distance to their off-the-beaten-path selection in motels in a town called Amherst was a necessity when it came to keeping Ben's picture out of the papers. Stopping at the Consumer's Beverages at the corner before heading to her room had added to the growing number of regrets on the night. The booze had done little to help her head. It had merely exacerbated the issue.

She had waited for Ben to stop over to apologize for what was said. Half of her understood the confusion and shock about what happened with Horace Waters. Ben had lost the opportunity for closure thanks to the man's suicide. His bitterness and the words that came with it were a reflex. They had been spoken in the heat of the moment, but they had been spoken nonetheless.

His doubts about the DSA matched those of Lincoln. The missing agent's pleas rang out in the darkness, trailing her every thought. She had attempted to track Lincoln down and bring him back into the fold. His fears over their department had over-shadowed his every move and her every intention. He couldn't trust in her because of the DSA. Ben appeared to feel the same. *Was* the DSA at fault? Had Morgan become blinded by loyalty? Those same self-doubts circled endlessly, much like Ben's question. One, in particular, had shattered the peace of their evening and divided them as a team. It was a question she should have considered long ago.

How do you see that ending for you, Morgan?

Every time she replayed the remark, her fists clenched tight to her side. She needed a release. Anger was a chemical reaction that demanded suppression, but it was controllable. That was where the booze had come in. She had drunk too much, too quickly, and it had offered little to assuage her bitter thoughts.

Morgan moved for the door. Sunlight reflected off the cracking mirror on the far side of the room and the peeling wallpaper across from it. The room would never have been considered high living, but the liquor bottle on the floor and the small puddle soaked into the carpet streaming from the lip did it no favors.

Her fury stuck with her. She held an unending annoyance at Ben's words, as well as at her own reaction. She had acted as if she had been scolded by a parent. More than anything, however, she was angry with her own actions in the matter. Was she wrong to have feelings for Zac? They rang true to her, the way his nerdy smile made her blush. Was she wrong to pursue him, to feel the connection she did with him? She had never wanted it to happen—not with anyone, let alone a colleague and friend. And now? She feared the end had come too quickly; she worried Zac's reticence after the briefing was more than maintaining the secrecy of their night of passion. Despite her intentions, her desires, Zac was slipping away.

Everything was slipping away.

The pounding returned, both at the door and in her head. Her hand rubbed her temple before reaching for the handle. The disgust returned as well, and she wondered what she would say to Ben and how to move forward with him as a partner. Only, it wasn't Ben at the door.

"Baxter?" Morgan asked, surprised at the sight of the mustached detective. "I thought—"

"Sorry to wake you," Baxter huffed.

"What's going on?"

He pointed inside the motel room. "Do you mind?"

"No. Of course not," she replied, puzzled by his concern. She stepped aside, kicking the clutter on the floor out of the way before he entered. Her entertainment from the previous night clanked along the floor and into the corner. "Come in."

Baxter stopped just inside the room and let the door close behind him. His eyes swept the wreckage. "Rough night?"

"Something like that," Morgan said. He stared at her for a long moment and she realized she was still wearing a tight t-shirt and shorts. Silently, she grabbed a pair of pants to slip on. "What's going on? I thought we were meeting with the medical examiner this morning?"

"We are," he confirmed. He kept his eyes away from the woman while she dressed. The act made her grin. She pulled an Orioles sweatshirt from her bag. As she straightened out the mismatched outfit, Baxter roamed the length of the room. The detective shuffled into the bathroom, hand always hovering over his holster. He returned after a brief moment. His next destination was the closet along the back wall, which he opened carefully. A content look spread on his face.

"Detective," Morgan called, patience fading fast. "I might be awake, but I get tired of guessing games."

"Sorry," Baxter said. "Just checking."

"Satisfied?" A chuckle escaped him and he nodded. Her hands remained locked on her hips. "Has there been another incident?"

Another nod. She didn't wait to follow up the question or bother to listen to a response. At the admission, Morgan snatched up her badge and sidearm. She slammed her feet into her boots and was out the door without another thought.

Two patrol cars sat in the parking lot outside her room. Lights flashed, doors opened, and the waiting officers held tight to their sidearms.

"What the hell?"

"Now, Agent Dunleavy—"

She shook her head and continued for the neighboring room. No matter what happened, no matter the rage still simmering from their time together the night before, Ben needed to be involved. Her hand hovered at his door, but Baxter stopped her.

"He isn't there."

"What?" Morgan backed away a step. Her gaze flitted between the closed door and the officers behind her as she faced the rosy cheeks of the detective once more. "How do you know?"

"When was the last time you spoke with your partner?"

Morgan stopped herself from saying his name, though the question took her off guard. "Not since about eight last night. Why?"

Baxter fixed his hair. He kept his eyes low, nervous about something.

"Detective?"

Baxter released a long breath. A hand raised and then lowered at the four officers locked and loaded for trouble. At his signal their weapons fell to their sides and they returned to their vehicles. The lights disappeared, the unspoken tension broken without another thought.

Morgan's eyes flared, demanding explanations from the somber officer. Baxter pointed to the empty, unmarked sedan at the end of the lot.

"You better come with me, Agent Dunleavy. You're going to want to see this."

CHAPTER FOURTEEN

Baxter remained tight-lipped the entire drive over from the motel. Morgan let her questions ruminate, and she breathed easier when the two extra squad cars departed in the opposite direction. Easier, but never completely comfortable with his silence.

No words were spoken on the subject. However, Ben had been mentioned though not by name. Had they figured out who her partner was? Were they hunting him as an escaped con with no idea about his affiliation with the DSA? And why were they keeping it a secret from her? Had she stepped into Baxter's unmarked sedan without realizing the danger?

When the car stopped in front of Sidelines, Morgan looked curiously over to her companion. "What are we doing here?"

Baxter exited the vehicle without a word. Morgan unclasped her seatbelt and followed him. He opened the door, though the sign in the window clearly read CLOSED.

The detective shifted aside and gave her access to the restaurant she had visited the night before. "We got the call around ten-thirty last night."

Tables had been upended throughout the dining area. Glass covered the floor. The scent of beer and booze filled the air. It sat in puddles on the floor, mixing with the melted snow from the late-night patrons. The television that had passed along the news of Horace Waters' demise lay on the bar, the screen cracked down the middle.

Morgan stopped inside the entrance, mouth agape. "What the hell happened here?"

"You tell me."

The thin stalk of the manager rushed toward her. The nervousness from her questioning the previous night was no longer present, and the man's face was flush with anger.

"Excuse me?" Morgan asked. She loomed over him.

"You were with him," Manfredi shot back and his finger stabbed the air in front of her. "That lunatic. Just look at this place!"

Baxter cleared his throat as he shuffled between them. "Mr. Manfredi? Please let us handle this."

"So handle it," Manfredi spat at the rotund officer. "Arrest her and her nutso of a partner and be done with it."

Oh, hell, Morgan thought, finally understanding Baxter's search of her room as well as the backup on hand. "My partner did this?"

Baxter shifted away from the fuming manager, waving Morgan to follow. "Come on, Agent." He pointed to the corners of the room and the security cameras she had failed to consider during their visit. Footage could identify Ben if seen by the wrong person. She held her breath, sticking close to her escort. Baxter led her toward the back of the sports bar. "Cameras caught most of it. Gotta love the security-conscious public."

"Sure," she muttered. Her eyes scanned the room once more, taking in the destruction being laid at the feet of her partner. If they realized from the footage who they were dealing with, the smashing up of some local bar was going to be the least of her worries. Morgan couldn't help wondering if she might have prevented it all if she had stayed and talked things out with him—worked through his overwhelming emotions over the death of Horace. She had been angry, though, both at his bitterness and his accusations. She had left, giving them both the space necessary to deal with things.

Morgan's head remained low when she entered the cramped closet or, as the door indicated, the *Security Suite*. Manfredi barreled through them, huffing with each step. His shoulder slammed into her side without a word of apology. The bitter little man sat in front of the console with a large grimace on his face. Four screens displayed the cameras in the main dining area. Another console to the right kept an eye on the grounds surrounding the business, including the thin alley at the rear.

"All right," Baxter said, hand on the back of Manfredi's chair. "Play it back for her."

The live feed cut out and a recording took over. His irritated breath quieted allowing Morgan a clear picture of the bar from the night before. The time stamp in the lower corner displayed that the footage took place a little after ten.

The incident started with a single patron. Excited to meet a larger group at the end of the bar, he failed to notice Ben's slumped shoulders leaning back from his stool. He must have relocated there after her departure. A small, innocuous collision occurred, sending Ben's half-guzzled beer out of his grasp to the floor below. Apologies were given, and the patron's hand quickly shifted for his wallet while waving the bartender down for a replacement.

The apology and the charity, unfortunately, were not accepted. Not by a long shot. Ben's hand slapped the money to the ground. As the young man turned to confront the unnecessary act he was met with Ben's fist square against his right cheek. The man fell and failed to get up.

The larger group waiting for the newcomer looked on in astonishment, then appeared to remember their brotherly code. They rushed the lone figure in black, who greeted them eagerly. Ben ducked the first assailant before he tackled the second into a nearby table, shattering it into splinters. A bottle smashed against the back of Ben's head, but it seemed to do nothing. He spun wildly, decking a young lady without thought. He was already moving for another pair of men, ready to mix it up with anyone and everyone in the place.

Morgan's unease increased. Neither Baxter nor Manfredi made a comment about the footage or the image of the man at the center of the melee. They made no mention of the man's name—her partner's identity. She had given them the alias Zac had worked up the day before in case questions arose, and it appeared to be holding, though with each punch thrown she questioned how much longer it could.

Soon the bar was empty of conscious patrons. Only the groans of the fallen and the rage of the man in the middle of the brawl remained. Ben screamed in a voice Morgan had never heard before. He didn't even look like himself, but a dark reflection of the man she had come to know.

"Stop it," she said, head twisted away in disgust.

Baxter blocked the feed for her. "If we hadn't already called you in about a number of these reports I'd say your partner has quite a temper."

Morgan stopped. That specific thought hadn't occurred to her, yet Baxter had recognized the truth immediately. He didn't know about Horace or what that event may have triggered in her partner. All he saw was their open case involving innocent people turning homicidal on their fellow man.

Morgan grinned to Baxter and slapped his shoulder in thanks. Then she faced Manfredi, leaning over the small man. "Go back."

"Where?"

"How far back did you go?"

"Just to the incident," Baxter replied, brow furrowed. "Why?"

"Because I'm not covered in bruises and I was with him two hours earlier. Something happened to him here. And if it happened to him—"

"This might be where it happened to the others," Baxter finished, joining her at the chair.

Manfredi threw a questioning glance to the lead detective. Baxter rolled his finger and tilted his head to the feed. The crotchety manager sighed, and the footage skipped back through the previous evening.

It went quick. Morgan's eyes scanned the scene rapidly until a shadow at the corner booth caught her attention. "Right there."

Manfredi stopped the feed at the perfect moment. A man approached Ben from behind, something small wrapped tightly in his hand.

Baxter inched toward the screen, squinting hard. "Is that a needle?"

The injection occurred quickly, as did the effect on its target. Ben's movements faltered, and his head lowered toward the table. The man that stuck him with the needle took a moment to gloat while he sat on the far side of the booth directly in view of the camera.

"It can't be," Morgan said, the wind knocked out of her.

"Agent Dunleavy?" Baxter asked. He pointed at the figure filling the monitor. "You know this guy?"

"Yeah. I know him." Her words were lost on the image. Lost on the past. "But he's…"

He's dead.

"Who is he?"

Morgan hesitated, staring at the man on the screen. His mannerisms differed, but the face was the same. It was the face of a man who had died three months earlier in an electronics store in Bellbrook, Ohio.

"His name is Clevinger. Howard Clevinger."

CHAPTER FIFTEEN

Sweat pooled along Ben's brow. He wiped it away only to have it replaced in seconds in a steady flow. The swelling heat centered on the small circular puncture mark at the back of his neck and spread out to every inch of his body. Blood boiled in his veins. His heart pounded in his ears. Every noise was a crash, every whisper a scream; his senses were on overload.

Rocking back and forth along a park bench, Ben watched in silence. Two men loitered outside a bank on Grant. They laughed, told stories, and yelled at cars that blew through the stop sign at the corner. Every motion, every expression, was caught by his bloodshot eyes.

Through a red haze, Ben grabbed the Ruger at his side and tucked it close, keeping the weapon hidden beneath a newspaper. The clip unloaded, and the clicking sound caused him to reach for his ear in pain. There was a full clip, the same as had been present mere minutes earlier. Still, he checked; the act was necessary.

He circled the area for hours in wait. It had been a long night out in the cold, though he barely even noticed the freezing temps anymore. Heat rose from the back of his neck, though the wound's origin had slipped away as easily as the hours of darkness in the city of his birth. Despite the late hour something kept him going, even as his eyes fought to relax; a need pushed him forward.

You're angry, a voice called to him—the shadow from the bar. It had done something to him, injected him with something. The substance had been the answer he had come back to Buffalo to find, wasn't it? A haze fell over Ben's mind; a cloud set him on edge, and his nerves felt overloaded and frayed. His rocking increased on the bench, his gaze locked on his targets.

Don't let go of the anger. Use it. Use it like you never have before.

The two men, despite their security uniforms, hooted and hollered at a pair of women walking down the block. The young ladies blushed, while moving slightly faster at the same time. The men tracked the pair until the corner, their leering gaze carrying nothing but arrogance. They owned the place. They owned everyone in their small playground. That was their perspective.

It was Ben's as well.

You have been wronged. Make it right.

He knew the men from his time on the beat. They were former cops, pretentious enough to believe they stood above the law: that the city served them instead of the other way around. When it had become clear the job entailed actual work, that there was no golden parachute in their future, they had moved to a simpler life. Security gigs and mediocre positions. Less life threatening, and much more attuned to their desires.

Make them suffer, the voice beckoned. Ben's rocking continued, and his head throbbed from the sleepless night. Now that he was outside the law and away from the rules set forth by his former career, he could make things right.

Both men were former associates of Horace Waters. Horace, the man responsible for Ben's exile, was dead. Every question about the incident, however, remained an open page in the book of Ben's life. Each one was a haunting reminder. He refused to allow them to dog him for the rest of his days.

After his fall from grace, Ben had looked them all up. He had researched them. He knew their names, the names of their children and parents, their home addresses, and their credit scores. During his trial, however, there had been no way to act on the information. There had been no way to ask the questions never mentioned during his legal farce.

Make them all pay.

Now there was the unrelenting need and the opportunity. Ben required answers, and they all lay with the men across the street. He swiped at the sweat coating his frozen skin. After checking the Ruger once more—satisfied at the full clip and the bullet in the chamber—Ben gazed at the sun inching toward the western horizon.

Questions remained, and they were going to be answered. The final words of the voice from the bar rang in his ears.

No matter the cost.

CHAPTER SIXTEEN

All sense left him. All manner of breath escaped his lungs, and he couldn't catch it no matter the effort. Zac rushed down the sidewalk, skirting the pedestrians who sluggishly walked away their lunch hour on the cold afternoon in downtown Bethesda. Apologies were thrown mindlessly, his focus on the tiny bistro at the corner.

She had called him an hour earlier. A hushed tone offered the invite. He had barely heard another word after that, his concern firmly on the reason behind the request. It was a surprise, to be sure. His work days had become long, drawn-out battles between the professional and the personal. The line blurred, though Zac always let work overcome all else. Handling the operational support of the field team's current situation in Buffalo was like an out-of-body experience to Zac, one he certainly preferred to the reality crashing down on him.

The door opened, and a dozen eyes were drawn to the panting young man with the thickening waistline letting the heat out of the place. She sat at the far end, an inviting look greeting him. Zac's feet shuffled through the thin layer of melted snow around the welcome mat.

Claire sat with her hands folded on the table. She wore a fleece sweater over jeans. She had never cared for the cold, preferring to bundle up with as many layers as possible to avoid the chill. Claire grinned at his approach and beckoned him to the small table in the corner of the bistro.

"Hey there," Zac's wife of six years said.

Zac stopped short of the table. He tried to catch his breath and cool down his body. Parking remained the eternal enemy of his lunch hour, and the time it took him to find a spot had been hastily made up for in his run. He paid for the exercise with a layer of sweat that soaked his clothes.

"Hey," he mouthed, trying to slow his heart rate. "What's going on? Are you all right? Is it Alex? Is he okay?"

"He's fine," Claire said as she stood. Her hand slowly guided him to the seat across the table. "We're all fine. Alex is with my mother. Breathe."

Zac nodded, glancing around the room. The stares had faded from his auspicious entrance into the bistro and returned to their own conversations and meals. Zac lifted his computer bag over his shoulder and parked it next to his chair. Sitting uncomfortably, he snatched the complimentary water from the table and downed half the glass. He placed the plastic cup back on the round tabletop. His eyes impatiently waited for more from his wife.

"What's going on, then?" he asked, sharper than he'd intended.

"Oh." Her eyes fell at the question. "Well, you've been so busy with work, and I had some time, so I figured we could get lunch."

"Really?" She laughed at his reaction, and her hand fell on his. A meal together? Was it such a foreign concept that he had assumed the worst?

"Yes," Claire said. "Really."

Zac settled on his chair. "How did you even find out about this place?"

"I found some receipts," Claire said. "Thought it would work."

Zac grinned. He had been ordering from the bistro regularly over the last year. They made a steak-and-cheese sandwich like nobody else in the area. It tasted like his mother's. She always made it for Zac when his father went away on business. Just the two of them. That had been one of the few quality moments they shared together—being honest with each other and true to themselves.

"My wife, the covert agent," Zac said. Claire beamed at the compliment. Flushed cheeks against her pale skin brought back memories to the overworked DSA tech. She looked radiant, just like she had when they met in college. They had discussed so many plans for the future back in those days. They talked about careers, a home, and starting a family.

Claire leaned back against her chair. Her arms stretched out before her, fingers positioned like a gun. "Modine. Claire Modine."

Zac's eyes fell away, his hands pulling back from the table. He wanted to laugh. He wanted to sit with his wife and tell jokes and devour all he had missed over the last few weeks during his self-exile from the world. He wanted to ask about her day, to ask her how she was feeling. Winter always brought on headaches for her. Did she need anything for the house? Was everything still in working order?

He knew the answer. For Zac, working order had flown out the window and would never come around again. His entire equilibrium was lost thanks to his work at the DSA, and the woman behind his troubles.

Morgan.

A look of concern took over Claire's entire face. She didn't know, couldn't understand, what he had done. The why of it all. How could she when even he failed to grasp the subject. Sure, there were some clear reasons behind the affair: the need for companionship, and the need for excitement beyond the mundane nature of domesticity. Once he believed Claire had been enough to fulfill him. He wanted those bygone days back.

"Everything all right?" Claire asked. She tried to cut through the veil of silence he had placed between them.

With a single question Zac realized the concern on her face existed for a reason. Of course she was concerned. Her husband was never around. He thought she had no idea, but how could she not? It was in the simple request for a lunch date that he couldn't fathom. She missed him. He missed her as well, but his secrets weighed him down—his inability to stay true to a simple promise he had once made. It was a promise he still wore on his finger. Claire wasn't clueless, but she didn't know either. Not the details. Not everything.

Zac fought to speak, wondering what to tell her—how to open up to her without releasing the floodgates. Instead, he forced a thin smile. "It's nothing."

"Work?"

Something like that, he thought before answering with a vague,

"Always."

Claire pointed to the door. "We could always forget about lunch…"

Zac waved her off. "Work can wait."

He took her hand. It was soft and warm, melting his cold skin. The bistro fell away until there was only them.

"Are you sure?"

"Very," Zac said. They pulled apart when the waiter moved for the table. "Thank you for this."

Their waiter entered into their private lunch date, offering daily specials as well as his joke of the afternoon. Zac politely chuckled through the exchange, watching his wife the entire time. Every smile was a dagger in his heart—a constant reminder of what he had done. He continued to hurt her every moment the secret remained hidden.

Yet, he couldn't stop thinking about Morgan. Her lips. Her body. Every sound. Every touch. No matter what Sullivan said about the woman, he continued to think about her and their night together. In the deputy director's eyes, Morgan had betrayed the DSA and, in turn, Zac. He tried to let it go, to let *her* go. He needed to for the sake of his entire world.

For Zac, everything came down to wants and needs. Morgan—the one he wanted: excitement and the ultimate fantasy to combat his banal existence. Claire—the one he needed: the safety and security of his family, the warmth of their love for each other. *What mattered more?*

Zac fell silent, the answer hidden deeper than the secret separating him from the world.

CHAPTER SEVENTEEN

Sullivan laughed. A boastful, jubilant guffaw swelled from his throat and escaped into the open air of the lunchroom. Heads turned. Some offered curious stares while other wide-eyed subordinates joined in on the affair.

Contentment suited him. Even surrounded by dullards, analysts with little in the way of talent outside the ability to shuffle a mouse around a screen, Sullivan grinned and joked. He listened to their tales, their great adventurous commute from the suburbs or the technical difficulties thanks to a network outage for thirty minutes during the ten o'clock hour.

Insipid and meaningless drivel, yet he buried all deprecating comments. Right now, he needed them on his side. From William in Support to Jennifer in Operations, he required dozens of commoners for his cause. And with the day's events sealing away any unspoken questions, thanks to his quick decision to silence Horace Waters, Sullivan was well on his way to gaining everything he had worked for.

When the phone rang his grin widened. The day swung in his favor, and nothing could change that. The story of the jammed printer—a disgusting waste of time—faded behind the ringing of the small device in Sullivan's hand. He accepted the call without a glance at the ID.

"More good news?" Sullivan asked.

"Was it you?"

The question was sharp, and it snapped Sullivan from the mutterings of the rabble surrounding the table. The deputy director offered a slight nod and a smile to his subordinates before shuffling his chair away and standing. His lunch suddenly disagreed with him. The man on the other end of the line had that effect on most people.

"Donald?"

Donald Stallworth was his colleague at the NSA and the one man working with him in the background. Stallworth was always a hard man to pin down, one without natural drive. He had simply fallen into his position of power and learned to clutch it tightly in his sausage-like grasp rather than try to achieve more.

"Was it you?"

"I... Yes, Donald," Sullivan stammered at the harsh edge to his friend's voice. It took a moment to remember they were not equals in the endeavor; Stallworth's influence and resources were a necessity for the work ahead. "Waters knew too much. He had to—"

"Ah," Stallworth interrupted. "I just heard about Buffalo."

"I was going to inform you at our next meeting," Sullivan lied. It was a nasty habit he had formed with the man. Sullivan tired of explaining events as they happened. He preferred to listen to the mundane complaints from his subordinates than the wheezing breath of the behemoth on the other end of the line at times.

"After the fact," Stallworth grumbled.

"Unavoidable. The timetable—"

"Is precisely what I'm calling about. I want to hear it from you now. Were you involved?"

"Excuse me?" Sullivan asked. He rounded the corner out of the lunchroom then tucked in the shadowed end of the corridor away from listeners. "I'm afraid I don't—"

"I can't imagine you would go ahead without informing me beforehand," Stallworth said, inattentive and gnawing on something as he spoke. "We've spoken about the logistics required, and now that word has gotten out to the other members of the group it is too late to put the genie back in the bottle."

"Donald..."

"There were always going to be risks, but this? Dammit, Greg—"

"Stop talking, Donald," Sullivan boomed. "What are you saying?"

"The plan," Stallworth said. "It can't be done. It's over. If we're smart we can contain the damage before we're noticed by the group."

"What does Waters' death have to do with—?"

"Not that pissant pawn. You think his miserable existence means anything to our doomed plan?"

"You keep saying that, Donald," Sullivan said, his voice slow and calm; the effort to console the man was a chore. "The plan is fine. The plan is—"

"Over," Stallworth snapped. "Hollis called me this morning in a rage. He's demanded a nationwide hunt, and wants to utilize resources from every available agency tucked in the Trust's pocket."

"Why? What's happened?"

"The Wellspring is missing."

"No."

They had lost the trail of the enigmatic weapon, the heart of his ambition, in Buffalo. He had spent months researching to find any trace of the tool—one that was central to the future of the DSA. The Wellspring was crucial to all his ambitions. There had been months of planning and probing, of manipulating those around him and threatening all who stood in his way. The contentment of only moments ago dissipated like a stiff wind.

Sullivan leaned along the wall, his weight suddenly too heavy to carry without the assistance. Stallworth continued to grumble through the line.

"Now, I believe if we work quickly we can minimize the risk to our positions and our lives. There are certain precautions in place to block our direct involvement."

The safe path—it was the only one the belligerent bureaucrat followed. Sullivan had used the same approach in the past and it never got him anywhere. He was ostracized from public service, a leper on the national scene. He had been relegated to a windowless office in a warehouse for has-beens and nobodies.

No more, the man cried in his turbulent thoughts. It was time to throw away safety and take the risk.

"Do you hear me, Greg?" Stallworth said. "It's over and you need to accept that so we can—"

"No," Sullivan said, silencing the man. "We continue as discussed."

"Greg?"

"They no longer have the Wellspring, Donald. The path is clear for us. We can't delay." If the Wellspring was indeed in the open then the services of the DSA had become more vital than ever; their connections to the various law enforcement departments allowed a treasure trove of information to pass between their walls. All they required was the proper motivation and the correct leadership. This was not the time to surrender the fight. This was the time to *strike*. "We accelerate our plans."

"The risks —"

"Are nothing compared to the rewards," Sullivan finished. "Metcalf knows where the Wellspring is. I'm sure of it. Reach out to the Council, Donald. It's time to remove her from the DSA. This is our chance at last."

My chance. This is my chance to change the future. My chance to change the world, to make history by altering the course of human destiny forever.

The smile returned to Sullivan's lips. "No one will take it from us."

CHAPTER EIGHTEEN

Sparks flew between the wires. There was a flicker, and then nothing, followed quickly by another. The panel scraped along his wrists as Ben tapped the pair of electrical wires between his fingers. There was another spark, the dim light of success before darkness returned to the sedan. The wind howled through the broken window as cries rose from nearby apartments. None were aimed in his direction, the lack of an alarm maintaining the silence of his actions.

Perseverance won out. The spark grew under his ministering, and the engine roared to life. Ben laughed, the deep sound booming in the cabin of the stolen vehicle and echoing into the night. He tied off the wires and secured the panel. Ben's gaze trailed up the block and his waiting target. The headlights blazed and the engine screamed his arrival.

"Whoa! Whoa!"

The shouting came from a bystander across the street. Ben slammed the accelerator to the floor. The stolen Buick, well past its prime, barreled toward the unsuspecting target.

"Look out!" the bystander bellowed. His cries caused the off-duty security guard to finally take notice. The guard veered from the sidewalk at the sight of the Buick bearing down on him. Ben tucked low behind the wheel. The front tires bounced from the impact of the curb. The guard jumped out of the way of the speeding vehicle. He rolled along the ground into an alley adjacent to the building. The car continued until crashing into the side of a stoop leading to an apartment building.

Ben staggered from the Buick. The impact had caused a large cut above his left temple. His target paused near the corner of the block for a look at the crash.

"What the hell is wrong with you?" the guard called as he got to his feet. Ben recognized him from the files. Jamar Price—Horace's former partner on the force. Ben answered with the Ruger in his hand.

"He's jacked on something!" a pedestrian shouted. Concern rang in his voice, but the glint of the pistol caused him to flee from the scene before Ben's full attention turned in his direction.

"Hey, man, just back off," Jamar said. His hand shifted slowly for the holster beneath his jacket. "This doesn't have to get ugly."

"I think it does," Ben answered as he leveled the Ruger at the man.

Jamar hesitated, then fled around the side of the apartment building and away from the flickering headlights of the crashed car. Ben let him fade into the growing shadows of the night, content to follow at his own pace.

This was his home, *his* neighborhood long before it had belonged to men like Jamar Price. He recognized the block from when he worked the beat and knew what barred the guard's escape route. The alley was attached to a block of closed businesses. For security measures and the safety of their clientele the locals had installed a fence to separate the alley from the residential area to the rear. People passing through had to climb a ten-foot-tall chain-link barrier or walk around the block.

Jamar strained to climb the fence. Blood dripped from his scraped fingers down the chain-link. He made it halfway before he slipped. He fell hard against a pile of snow and refuse buried in the alley. When he started for a second attempt, Ben was waiting.

He lifted the tall, slender man by the collar, then dropped him back into the pile of filth. The impact stole the man's breath, and Jamar's head hit against a nearby trash can hard. The shaken guard reached for his pistol and freed it from the confines of his holster. Ben's foot collapsed on the man's wrist and the weapon skittered across the alley. Panicked, Jamar leapt after it, only to see his path barred by the looming shadow of his attacker. Ben lifted him to his feet before pushing him against the rattling fence.

"Hey, man," Jamar pleaded. "I got cash. Whatever you

need."

"Answers," Ben heard himself growl in a voice he failed to recognize.

"Huh?"

Ben brought the butt of his Ruger down on Jamar's shoulder. Rather than let him fall back to the ground, the furious agent's hand held tight to Jamar's collar to keep him trapped against the fence.

"Horace Waters."

"Horace?" Jamar asked in confusion. He raised his hands in defense. "Horace croaked. Reaper got him. Not me. I didn't…"

A fist slammed into Jamar's stomach. "Shut up. He took my life. Why?"

"How would I—?"

Ben screamed as he tossed the frightened guard to the ground. He holstered the Ruger and clenched his fists. He didn't want the weapon to interfere with his pleasure at beating the truth from Jamar.

"Wait," Jamar yelled at his approach. "Wait!"

Ben didn't listen. He kicked Jamar in the side. Something cracked under the weight of his boot. Joy spread across Ben's face.

"You're going to need a doctor, Jamar," Ben sneered. "Or a coroner. Up to you."

Through the beaming moonlight in the alleyway, Jamar's eyes widened with recognition. "You. I know you. But you're locked up."

"Not right now I'm not," Ben said. He slammed Jamar against the cold brick of the apartment building. "Now tell me."

"What?" Jamar's eyes watered. "Tell you what, man?"

"Why did he ruin my life? He framed me for something I never did. Why? Who hired him? Tell me!"

"I—"

"Tell me!" His anger roared over the sound of traffic from down the street and the blaring sirens racing toward their location. Ben let the injured man drop from his grip. Jamar's tall frame slid along the building's surface and to the cold concrete beneath. When the bleeding figure looked up to his assailant he was met with a close-up of the man's sidearm.

"I don't know," Jamar said. "It was all Horace!"

The Ruger lit up the alley. The bullet shattered the brick near Jamar's face. The cringing man dabbed at his cheek, where blood ran from a large gash.

"You're lying," Ben growled. "Someone sent him after me. Someone wanted me to take a fall and he made it happen. Who was it?"

The Ruger inched closer to Jamar's face. He raised his hands in defense once more. Blood mixed with the cold sweat covering his dark skin.

"Listen," he started, panting with each breath. The cracked rib put a strain on every word. "There was a guy."

"A name. Now!"

"Some guy," Jamar replied. The gun moved closer. Jamar closed his eyes tight. "An older guy! Said you saw something you shouldn't have, something about that place on Wex and some dude you chased in there. He wanted to make sure you paid for sticking your nose where it don't belong. I told Horace he was a fool for even thinking about working with the guy. He never listened. He was always trying to make a name for himself, no matter what lines he had to cross. But Horace figured things out real quick after he killed the dude and burned you for it. They tried to take him out, so he ran and hid. Horace tried to call me once, but I hung up. Wanted nothing to do with it. That's all I know. That's all!"

The cold metal of the gun pressed into Jamar's flesh. "Then we're done here."

"Hey, man. Come on now." Tears flowed from the broken and bleeding man. The trigger tightened under the weight of Ben's finger. Excitement filled the agent's eyes.

"Riley!" The cry shattered the silence of the moment. Ben whirled about, gun raised.

Morgan stood at the mouth of the alley, sidearm drawn on him. "Move away from him. Slowly."

"I'm saving you, dammit," Morgan said. She snatched his flailing arms and pinned them to the concrete. "Somehow I doubt you're seeing it that way."

"They took my life from me!"

"Maybe," Morgan replied, eyes pleading for him to listen. Behind them, footsteps boomed louder and closer. "Maybe they did, Ben. But they don't deserve to lose theirs. Not like this!"

"You don't know!" Ben yelled. His arms slipped loose from her grasp. He lashed out, hands knocking into her chest to force her off him. Her shoulder slammed hard on the pavement from the impact. Whatever caused his rage, whatever was part of the injection he received, it seemed to dull his pain as well as his other senses.

He stumbled for his gun while she jumped to her feet. "Ben, listen to me. You've been drugged. This isn't you. Think about it. At the bar. The needle in your neck. You felt it. It was the drug. The one we came to stop. Do you remember?"

He shook his head and pointed to the fence. "Why are you helping him?"

"I'm helping you!" she exclaimed. He continued for the gun. Her own was tucked close, finger tensed along the trigger. One shot and it would be over, but so would be her chances of saving him now that the police were at the end of the alley. Her finger slipped from its position, slim hope barring her from acting. "Think about it, Ben. Just think about it. At the bar? It was Clevinger."

Ben bent to retrieve the Ruger. The silence in his movements gave her pause. She lowered her pistol and moved toward him.

"He's dead."

"I know," she said. His head slumped to his chest, his back to her. She approached with slow and calm steps. Behind her, voices from the front of the building filled the air. The gunshot had drawn their attention. She reached out to him. Time fought against her as much as her partner. "Yet I saw him. I don't get it, but Howard Clevinger did this to you. I want to help. Please let me—"

His arm swung wide, his body spinning with it, until it connected squarely above her left eyebrow. Morgan tumbled to the pile of garbage along the side of the building. A deep laceration grew thick with blood from the ass end of his Ruger.

"No!" His shadow loomed over the dazed agent. "You're trying to stop me. This is my chance to find out the truth. I have to know why this happened to me."

Ben's hand shook with the Ruger in his grip. His eyes blinked rapidly, unable to focus. The drug threatened to burn him out. It would succeed if he pulled the trigger.

"Ben, I..." She struggled to find the words, her head throbbing. "I get how important this is. I do. We'll figure it out, but only *after* we get you help. You're sick. You're..."

He tucked the Ruger away, which gave Morgan pause. Sadness filled his eyes for a brief flicker. There was a concern in his brown orbs that burned away in an instant with the rush of footsteps echoing closer. Radio chatter accompanied the approaching shadows. The police were on their way.

Any chance of understanding faded in an instant, and the rage returned. His arm shot out, slamming against her left side. She curled up as the breath was forced from her body. When she dipped, a second blow struck out against her bloodied brow. Her body flopped to the pavement, her vision doubled and fading to black. All that remained in view were the stripes of Ben's sneakers in front of her. All she heard was his voice railing against her pleas.

"You sent them after me!"

"I... I didn't..."

"Stay down, Morgan," the infected agent begged through clenched teeth. "Stay the hell down. I'm done with your lies."

"Ben, I..." Morgan fought for her knees. Her hands clamped along her side. The merest touch sent waves of agony throughout her body. Her head lolled to her chest and felt like a lead weight. Propped with her knees under her, she glimpsed her partner on the other side of the fence. In the thickness of the night he fled, becoming another shadow in the city.

"Dammit."

"Ma'am, is everything...?" a voice called from behind. "Agent Dunleavy?" Baxter helped her to her feet, the world spinning. "We need to get you to a doctor."

"No." She waved him off. She held fast to the nearest wall, cradling her ribs. "Medical kit in the car."

"You might have—"

"I know what I might have, Detective," she wheezed, regretting the sharpness of her words. Her eyes softened, trailing back to the departing shadow of her partner. "Just like I know what he definitely has. And it sure as hell isn't time."

CHAPTER TWENTY

The door slid open with a hiss, letting Morgan into the vacant offices of the Chief Medical Examiner. The late hour explained the emptiness of the space. The temporary entry code offered with unwavering trust by Baxter, even after the night's events, allowed her unfettered access. The late hour was also a necessity, since most of the day had been spent hunting for her partner.

Thinking of Ben brought back a wave of pain. Her brow had been stitched haphazardly in the rearview mirror of the rental car. Baxter had provided a second pair of eyes and hands in case she passed out. Her shoulder still ached from its collision with the pavement. Her left arm pleaded to rest. Her ribs joined the chorus; they had been bandaged hastily to hold them in place. Suffice it to say, Morgan desired little more than sleep and recuperation. A day off would have been nice, for sure. More than anything, though, she wanted Ben back safe and sound.

But where to start? Ben's deterioration was clear. The speed at which his rage took over was incredible. From the bar fight to the alley, little remained of the man's true nature. His anger was a guided missile with one clear goal: find answers relating to what Horace did to him. If not for Baxter's arrival, Morgan wondered if she would still be alive — afraid of the answer.

The medical examiner's reports flooded the room. A small desk was buried under lab results, tucked beneath mountains of pending avenues of research. No clear line of thinking surfaced. Additionally, there was no exact science of where to go or how to crack whatever was injected into the bloodstream of seven people in the last two weeks to cause them to commit murder.

Morgan took a deep breath. Her pained eyes read the small

printed pages that had been strewn around the room like confetti. She needed to focus. She needed to find the solution. Tonight. Now. It had been twenty-four hours since Ben's injection.

An injection which had come from Howard Clevinger.

The name stopped her. *How? How could it be him?* When she had last laid eyes on the man sporting the numbers two and eight in deep scars across the backs of his hands, Lincoln had put three bullets in his chest. The final survivor of the Bellbrook debacle had died before he completed the transformation that had sentenced the rest of the town to death.

The how of it all started and ended with a dead man, but it led her to another question unable to be answered by the reports. *Why?* Not just the ethical question. She understood evil existed in the world. People did horrible crap to each other every day. But why Buffalo, and why at this exact juncture? Why specifically target each of the victims? The simple questions baffled her and everyone else working the case. There appeared to be no goal behind the actions. Unless that was the desired outcome, which meant there would be no reasoning with the madman.

"It just *can't* be Clevinger," Morgan said. Her hand slammed hard against the desk. The pain reverberated down her arm, joining the tingling sensation of her shoulder and the throbbing of the cut along her temple. "It can't be. That crazy bastard is dead."

Reaching for the report on the first victim, the name Ben had recognized from the briefing—Ritchie—Morgan stopped. The pitter-patter of feet traveled down the entrance hallway to the office. Morgan's hand glided to her hip and the pistol tucked in its holster. The Glock greeted the shadow in the doorway.

"Bastard is a little harsh," the shadow announced.

When he stepped out of the darkness into the room proper, Morgan's sidearm nearly slipped to the floor. He looked different than she remembered. He was no longer shrouded in desperation. The man before her held his head up high with confidence. He opened his winter coat to show its emptiness. A larger-than-necessary bow tie above a brown vest completed the look.

"What did you to do to Riley?"

"Nothing," he said. Even his voice was different. It was stronger; more together than the man she had met previously.

The man shot to death by Lincoln. He hesitated at the sight of the weapon poised to fire. "I swear."

Morgan's head ached. Her eyes watered from the pain of her struggle with Ben. Her vision blurred, and her feet felt unsteady beneath her. They threatened to collapse as easily as her sanity at the sight of the dead man in the room.

"Bull," she spat. "I saw the feed from the bar. You injected him with whatever is making people go crazy. I want to know how to stop it. Now!"

Clevinger's eyes were soft and disarming. "It wasn't us, Agent Dunleavy."

"Us?"

Behind Clevinger, two shadows took form in the doorway. Both carried the same build as the man in the center of the room. Each stood unique in small respects, namely their gait and manner of dress, but as they stepped into the dim light of the office both looked very much like the man already standing before a suddenly overwhelmed Morgan Dunleavy.

Two more Howard Clevingers.

"Us."

CHAPTER TWENTY-ONE

"Don't move. Any of you."

The medical examiner's office had been her refuge—a place to take stock and figure out her next move in order to cure her partner of the affliction that was sending him on a crash course with the great beyond. According to the security footage from the sports bar one man was behind the string of random murders in the Nickel City. He was a killer without physically committing the act. Howard Clevinger. It was a simple explanation; well, maybe not simple considering the man had taken three bullets to the chest in Bellbrook, but the footage gave her a suspect.

Then *they* walked in the room: three more versions of the man. Each one carried the same face, albeit with small caveats. Two wore glasses, one thick-rimmed and sliding from the bridge of his nose, the other with thin rectangular lenses stretching the width of his face. The third—the first to enter the room—wore none, and his gaze pleaded for a moment of her time.

"We didn't come to fight," the first Clevinger announced. Each held their hands before them, open to denote their intentions. Morgan fought back a laugh. She had been in the presence of the man previously; she had seen what happened when she let her guard down around him. Yet these men weren't him. The differences were small, from the look in their soft eyes to their awkward stances. Even their style of dress was unique. Two wore business casual, one with a bow tie and vest, the other with a blue Stafford button-down. The figure nearest the door wore a *Tragically Hip* shirt under a leather coat.

Morgan hesitated, inching back to the nearest desk. With each step they closed the gap, three variants of the same man.

Her hand lightly touched the pulsing wound over her eyebrow. Was their presence a side effect of the blow from her partner? How was this possible?

"We came to help," the second man said. His voice mimicked the first. It was identical in accent and pitch.

"We have to stop him," the third one added in a more casual tone.

"Who?"

"Thirteen."

"Thirteen?"

They stopped in the center of the room. Glances were exchanged in silence, their hesitation palpable. An entire conversation went unspoken, shared in subtle shifts. Then they turned to her in unison. The image of six similar brown eyes cutting through the dim lights of the office frightened her. They kept their hands in front of them for her to see.

Each hand contained a similar scarring pattern. They were deep, self-inflicted in nature; each were in the form of a number. Sixteen. Seventeen. Eighteen. The Clevinger in Bellbrook carried the same scarring—a two and an eight. Twenty-eight.

"What are you?"

"Same as you, Agent Dunleavy," Sixteen replied.

Seventeen lowered his hands. "Our origins are simply—"

"Different," the man labeled as Eighteen finished.

Morgan let her weapon fall to her side. It slipped back against her hip, and she secured the Glock in her holster. She ran her hand along her chin, her tongue running along the front of her teeth. Her mind reeled, though the answer was emblazoned on their hands and in their mannerisms. Yet she held the notion back, hesitant to give it credence.

"And this other one?"

"Thirteen," the first Clevinger reminded her.

"Right," she said. "Thirteen. He's another you? Another Howard Clevinger?"

"Yes, but—"

"He's behind what's happening," she interrupted, her words cold. All three fell silent, peering at their neighbor for advice.

Sixteen rubbed the back of his neck nervously. "It's a bit embarrassing to admit."

"But yes," Seventeen joined his brother. He pushed his thick-rimmed glasses tight to his face.

The third shook his head and his arms crossed his chest. "Not a nice guy."

Morgan rolled her eyes. The pattern of conversation developed by the trio grated at her, yet she understood its development. There was comfort between them, a sense of belonging. It made her head hurt, but she recognized the advantages that came from speaking in shorthand knowing the other members of the threesome would finish the thought with ease.

They were the same, yet in two specific circumstances Morgan had witnessed a version of Howard Clevinger very different than the three before her. The first in Bellbrook, labeled Twenty-Eight, had fallen to his own madness. Then there was the sadistic grin of the man on the sports bar's security footage. Thirteen.

"Why?"

"He enjoys it," Sixteen started.

"The chaos," Seventeen continued.

"The pain," Eighteen finished.

"We've been tracking his movements for months," Sixteen said. He sat along the edge of the table across from her.

"Very slippery," Seventeen commented.

"And clever," Eighteen pointed out. "Can't forget the cleverness."

"Clevingers," she uttered under her breath, running her hand through her hair. "You're clones. *Actual* clones."

Wholly functional humans born from the cells of an original host. The *real* Howard Clevinger. It remained a theory only, as the morality of it was too complicated to fathom. More recently the conversation had turned toward the medical and life-saving applications of the process for the original host. Again, they remained conversation pieces at stuffy conferences held in hotel ballrooms. No movement had occurred on the subject as far as she knew. Which it appeared was not much by the looks of the three fully-grown genetic miracles before her.

"We are," Sixteen said.

Morgan lifted her hands. "Not a sore subject, I hope. Do you have a problem with the 'C' word?"

"Do you?" Eighteen muttered, and his brother gave his arm a firm slap.

"Duly noted," Morgan said. "But how? And why?"

Sixteen shook his head. "Do you ask God why?"

"It simply is," Seventeen grumbled.

Eighteen fixed the collar of his leather coat. "He gave us life and a name."

"A number."

"True." Sixteen smiled, a hand to his chest. "Though I prefer Howie myself."

Seventeen waved from behind his brother. "Ward."

Eighteen threw a thin glare. "Clev."

"Clev?"

He shrugged. "Better than Inger."

"Poor Twenty-Two," Ward said with a laugh.

"He'll never live it down." Howie joined him. The same laugh echoed between the three of them.

"So you're normal? Or what passes for normal when it comes to Clevingers?" Morgan asked, pushing through the awkward question. Small, unsure nods escaped them. "But if you turn the clock back three slots we get an evil genius with a syringe?"

Howie sighed. He left the comfort of the desk to pace around the room as the other two iterations leaned on a nearby research table. "The progenitor tweaked the formula as he went."

"One through six were failures," Ward said, fixing his glasses. "Seven died of old age in a matter of weeks. Eight and nine fell in love and disappeared."

"So romantic," Clev cooed, the words filled with sarcasm.

"Ten, Eleven, and Twelve ran off after they were created. The progenitor was not getting the results he required. He needed us for his work, to help see new avenues of thought he could not process fast enough. So he toiled. He tweaked."

"A little too much," Clev added, pointing to his head.

Howie stepped in front of him. "Thirteen was the result. He changed things."

"Our creator witnessed the change," Ward explained. "He saw what Thirteen was becoming."

"Evil," Clev summarized.

"So he changed things again," Howie said without looking to his brethren. "Streamlined the process for efficiency. He focused on cognitive boosts and emotional stability."

Morgan held her tongue. The truth was insane, but it was standing in front of her. Clones. Each unique, each independent of the whole, but directed. Controlled and developed for a purpose. "He made you good guys."

Howie stopped, a thin smirk. "Mostly. There were some—"

"Odd ducks," Ward continued, tilting his head.

"Whackjobs," Clev clarified.

"I met one. Twenty-Eight?"

Their eyes illuminated at the mention of the man. Howie nodded. "Now we understand your first impression of us."

"I always said we needed better quality control," Ward said to the other two members of the trio.

Howie stopped him with a glare. "He was on our list to track down as well." He turned back to Morgan. "What happened?"

"He died," Morgan said, unable to look at them. The sound of gunshots still echoed in her memory. "Badly."

"Ah."

Ward shrugged. "Understandable."

"Complete and total whackjob," Clev reiterated.

"Why?" Morgan asked each of them in turn. "Why are you here? Shouldn't you be doing the work you were created for?"

"We tried," Howie said. "Our goals shifted."

"So did our creator's," Clev said with a snort. "When he abandoned us, we—."

Ward puffed his chest out in anger. "Now, we don't know—"

Howie stopped them. He cleared his throat, then fixed his bow tie. "Agent Dunleavy, you have to understand. Bettering the world is a worthwhile goal."

"One we believe in wholeheartedly," Ward confirmed.

"It was the *cost* we had a problem with," Clev muttered.

She had seen the work of two iterations tear apart the tranquility of the communities they had been unleashed upon. The science behind the signal in Ohio had taken the lives of seven thousand. Over the last two weeks more than a dozen people had met their end in Buffalo. Killer and victim alike ended up in the morgue. It was all because of a virus developed by one rogue Clevinger. Now another three versions of the man stood before her. Three more Clevingers who knew much more than they were saying. If she had additional time, if there was a way to both save Ben's life and pry the secrets from these men, she would. There wasn't. Not by a long shot.

"So you left?"

"Everyone has to leave the nest someday," Howie said.

"Even us," Ward confirmed with a smirk.

"Especially us," Clev finished.

"You came here to stop this?"

"We did," Howie replied.

"How?" Hope bloomed for the first time since learning of Ben's infection. As she scanned their faces, their eyes lowered to the floor. Hands retreated to their sides or deep within their pockets. "You don't know."

"Not yet," Howie started, finger raised.

"We haven't isolated the base components Thirteen is using to trigger the reaction," Ward continued. He circled around Morgan and headed for the paperwork littering the medical examiner's desk.

"Or the end result it causes," Clev finished, shuffling to join the two at the desk.

Morgan pulled the reports away from the curious trio, drawing back their wavering attention. "My partner is infected."

"Oh."

"We're... That is to say... Sorry," Ward said, stumbling over his words.

"Tough break," Clev said with a shrug.

"Shut it," she snapped to the leather-coat-wearing hardass. "You have to help me."

"Lady, there isn't—" Clev said. Ward dug his hand hard into his brother's shoulder.

"The time it would take..."

"We'll help," Howie announced. The other two huffed their displeasure then fell silent.

"Good," Morgan said. She handed the reports to Howie, who took them graciously.

"However, what my brothers say is true," he continued, passing the notes between them. "If your partner is infected with the virus we've estimated he only has forty-eight hours before system collapse."

Morgan looked to the clock on the wall. Half the night was lost, the rising sun mere hours away. Over a day had disappeared in her hunt for Ben.

"How long do we have?" Howie asked.

Morgan eyed each of them in turn, wondering how she could

put all her faith in Howard Clevinger. The Clevinger she met before had caused the deaths of thousands. Inadvertently, of course, but the science was his at the start. To trust these newcomers, brothers of the man, betrayed her sense of justice. It was a compromise against her entire being. She suddenly owed Lincoln an apology for not understanding his dilemma with a similar situation. The clock, however, was against her. There was no choice in the matter. She needed them.

"Agent Dunleavy?"

"We have less than eighteen hours."

CHAPTER TWENTY-TWO

Clarity. For Ben it struck the moment his vomit pooled around his fingertips. He had just finished heaving the last remaining contents of wings and fries left to him from the previous night. It ran down his blistered fingers, covering the small scrapes, before journeying to the pavement.

The truth had been right in front of him all along.

The night had been hard. He had scoured the streets for some sign of Jamar, while avoiding the growing presence of police. His objective needed completion and nothing would stand in his way.

He believed it to be the cause of his pulsing headache, once a dull thundering along his temple and now a repetitious drumbeat playing a solo against the entirety of his skull. The world turned red, flowing through his veins and swallowing the light all around.

Someone had hired Horace. Someone had sent him after Ben like a mad dog on a leash. Horace was the bullet, but someone else had pulled the trigger. Someone else had come up with the frame job. They had murdered the man Ben had chased into that house on Wex and pinned it on him. They took Ben's life in that moment as well.

The picture finally became clear as the dripping mass streaming for the storm drain at the edge of the sidewalk on the vacant block of the West Side. He suddenly understood the reason behind Horace's actions. Whatever Ben had stumbled upon at that house on Wex worried the figure tucked in the shadows, and Horace had acted on their behalf. Only one party stood out to win from his fall from grace.

The DSA.

More importantly, the woman in charge of the department: Susan Metcalf.

How could he not have seen it? Metcalf knew his entire life, every accomplishment, every failure, every lost opportunity. She knew everything.

Ben's bleeding knuckles paled. His fingers dug into the pavement of the alleyway. He screamed at his foolishness, at being so blind to the way his world shifted and the reasons behind it. The DSA had used him. It had started with Metcalf and Sullivan, then followed the chain of command down to the lowest levels.

That included Morgan.

The name stung when he thought of his partner. He had worked so closely with her for months. He had reached out to her as a friend, attempted to keep her safe from the threats internal and external. Yet through it all she had pushed him away, kept him at arm's length. She did so, while at the same time taking Modine into her bed?

She was manipulating them all.

It was all so clear to him now.

She laughed at him, sided against him to save the life of a scumbag like Jamar. He had demanded answers, yet she had stood in his way — an immovable impediment keeping him from closing the book on what had happened to him. The puppet masters behind the DSA manipulated his life and had done so for years.

She kept the truth from him.

No longer.

Ben stood, the remnants of puke dripping from his fingertips. He reeked. Vomit coated his hands and spread beneath his sneakers. He had not showered in two days, nor had he slept during that time. Not that the impetus to find a soft pillow and mattress had even entered his mind. Sleep was for other people. He had too much to do. His goal was in sight.

Metcalf remained out of reach, and his need was too immediate to risk the journey back to Bethesda. Also, she would never let the truth escape her lips. But someone else was here with him; that person had been an obstacle to his every move dating back to his arrival at the department.

Ben walked briskly against the winter wind, refusing to allow it to slow him down. When he reached the end of the block he was in a full run. In the back of his mind he heard the laughter of everyone that had toyed with him, that had kept secrets from him, like the rapid beating of the drum causing his world to bleed in red.

No longer.

He was going to get his answers, at any cost, from the one person left to him. That one person had proven herself to be nothing more than another betrayer—stabbing him in the back by refusing to understand his need, by hiding the truth from him when asked. It was a decision she would come to regret. Everyone would. But she would be the first.

It was time to pay Morgan a visit.

CHAPTER TWENTY-THREE

Hours slipped away. The sun waned overhead, fighting through the darkening clouds for scant moments before fading behind the skyline. Morgan hadn't seen the damn thing rise let alone set with the passing day. She stood, hands tucked inside the pockets of her black peacoat, in the doorway of a low-rent apartment on the outskirts of the city.

The medical examiner's office was not a viable location when it came to working with the three Clevingers. Though the building remained vacant for much of the night, the threat of being discovered was too great. Morgan thought about her motel room, the one blanketed with upended furniture, then put the notion away. Baxter knew where she stayed, and that little nugget might not play well with the secretive clones of Howard Clevinger.

Howie, the sixteenth iteration of *Clevinger Prime* as Morgan started thinking of him, knew a place. She was hesitant and their mode of transportation did not help win her over. The cargo van, spray-painted a light green that screamed of the Mystery Machine, choked exhaust and drifted haphazardly to the right; it made the trek an uneasy one even with Morgan following behind in her rental.

The apartment was small, though it held everything they required for further study. Microscopes. Spectrometers. Centrifuges. A fluorometer. There were at least a dozen other devices strewn throughout the six-hundred-square-foot space. She wanted to ask where it had come from, as well as what the hell they could have been doing with it all, but she stopped.

The work came first. It had to, for Ben's sake.

The M.E.'s reports offered a starting point and the three pseudo-geniuses went from there. Morgan tried to steer the ship as best as she could while fighting through the pain from her injuries and lack of sleep. Most of the conversation soared over her head. Years had passed since she last stepped foot in a research lab as anything other than an investigator. It had been longer since her doctoral work, though even then the theoretical side of things was never her strong suit.

The Clevingers handled the heavy thinking aspect of the debate. And it *was* a debate. There was yelling and fighting, both physical and verbal. Mostly, however, the tantrums wore on the exhausted and aching agent. She continued to press on, refusing to drown in their endless bickering. Her reflexive look to her watch every few minutes reminded her why. 4:46 pm. Less than six hours left to save Ben. Less than six hours to bring him back from the brink.

She hoped she wasn't too late.

What they determined in their search was how the act of murder triggered the collapse effect. While it was slower for some, the murderous act allowed the injected individual to settle down. That trigger started the chain reaction that ended their lives. Morgan could only pray Ben still wavered on the final deed.

"You're not looking at it right," Howie uttered, his face hidden behind one of the workstations in the far bedroom.

"We've been over this!" Ward bitched from behind the M.E.'s reports.

"Stop," Clev snapped. "Both of you. It's here. *This* is the key."

Morgan couldn't see what he pointed at next to the centrifuge. She didn't really care. The same argument had run for the last hour. It was filled with the directionless musings of intellectuals rather than solutions to the issue at hand. They were still at step one of the process: identification. Each step after that would take time — much more than they had left.

Morgan ran through it again without speaking, the mania of the Clevingers escaping her for the moment. On some level they knew what they were dealing with. An adrenaline cocktail sent the recipient into a rage spiral. As adrenaline increased, the frontal lobe should counteract the mounting anger with reason, but Thirteen's mixture prevented that from occurring.

The only thought left to the infected was rage. Literally lost to a sea of red, logic disappeared for the injected. In each case, every situation the victim-turned-killer found themselves in became one of increasing violence. Those murdered by the infected were more a victim of circumstance than anything else. It was a cumulative effect. Murder was the finale and their victims just happened to piss them off at the wrong time.

The question became how to counteract the drug? How to wipe away the cocktail handmade by a genius-level intellect like Thirteen and calm someone down? That had stood as the central argument for the last few hours.

Long past time for a change of tactics, Morgan slammed her hand on the desk. "Clevingers! Enough!"

All three stopped. Howie shuffled from his workstation to the main living space of the makeshift laboratory.

Clev was the only one not looking to the floor. "We have names, lady."

"Some better than others," Ward snickered.

"Hey," Howie exclaimed, slapping the air around Ward's arm.

"I like the name Howie," Clev said to his brother.

"You would," Ward laughed.

"Guys," Morgan said, cutting their latest distraction short. "I am armed. Work with me here."

"We are." Howie pinched the bridge of his nose. They all understood the stakes. Just as they understood the amount of time they had spent on the problem.

"This is taking too long."

"You want a miracle?" Clev started for her, but Ward held him back. "Dial the North Pole. Or how about you find Thirteen and ask him?"

"I have people working on it," Morgan said. She had wished for better news on that front as well. Baxter had put the city on high alert. Everyone hunted for Thirteen. Baxter had checked in at midday with nothing to report. Thirteen, from all appearances, was in the wind; the man had chosen to lie low, or perhaps he had vacated completely from the chaos he created.

"Great," Clev said exasperated. His hands flailed in the air, before shuffling off to the other side of the room.

"I guess it's back to tracking him down," Ward said. They

were curling up in defeat, surrendering. Morgan refused to let that happen.

"Not until we solve this," she said to Ward. "My partner's life is on the line. Tell me where we're at."

"That's hard to describe," Howie answered, though the words were slow. All three looked at each other; the answer was clear in their wavering glances. Nowhere.

"Try me."

Ward cleared his throat. "The issue is permanence. We've thought about sedatives as an option, but the rage induced by the virus — which we should really think about calling something else — would simply fight back to the point of death in the subject."

"Again, this is all speculation, since we have no way of knowing how anyone will react to this thing," Clev pointed out, the tone bitter and frustrated from the lack of results.

"He's right," Howie admitted. "Without a sample, we're —"

"Pissing in the wind," Morgan pressed. "Got it. Bastard's built his own failsafe into the vi… infection. Whatever."

Howie's hand fell on the reports. "We're talking about a re-wiring of the brain on a cellular level."

Ward nodded. "A controlled reaction with an uncontrollable response."

"I mentioned how not so nice Thirteen can be, right?" Clev said. He pulled a Yoo-hoo from a large cooler in the kitchen and popped the cap off.

Morgan ignored him and focused instead on the other two in the room. "Reason is shut off. The frontal lobe is bypassed. The amygdala is going off the scale. Blood vessels are constricting for an extended period. Sleep is out the window. Maybe he'll get some power naps, but actual rest?"

Howie tracked her train of thought. "He's burning out. Top to bottom."

"If he could understand that…" Ward stopped short, drawing the attention of the other pair of the trio.

"He can't. Remember?"

Ward waved him off, fighting for thought. "I know that, but if he —"

"Exactly," Morgan cried, the unspoken thought snapping like lightning between them. "Exactly!"

"I'm lost," Howie muttered. "I *hate* being lost."

Clev dropped the empty Yoo-hoo container on the table beside him. Chocolate liquid ran down his chin. "Oh. I see it."

"Liar," Ward chided.

"I do," Clev said. "If we…"

"It could…" Howie continued. He had picked up their train of thought.

"It will," Ward shouted with excitement.

"You've got it?" Morgan asked. Her heart pounded in her chest. Time ticked by. It had to work.

Clev nodded, pulling at the others toward the back room. "We do. Give us—"

Everyone in the room jumped when Morgan's phone rang. Her first thought went straight to Ben. She immediately found herself thinking he was better and their struggle was over. Those were perfectly reasonable thoughts. Unfortunately, the bubble burst. The caller ID displayed Metcalf's cell number.

Morgan groaned, then headed for the front door. She scanned the neighborhood, which was uncomfortably empty for the middle of the afternoon. She took a deep breath, letting the phone reach the fourth ring before clicking the accept button.

"Morgan here."

"I need an update," Metcalf demanded, sharp words booming through the speaker.

"We're working on it," Morgan answered, trying to be as vague as possible. It had been her responsibility to keep Ben in check during the operation, forcing him to remain by her side their entire visit to prevent him being recognized. Now, not only was he loose in the city, but he was also a threat to anyone he came across.

"I tried Agent Riley," Metcalf said. "There was no answer."

Morgan hesitated, turning back to the three working individuals in the back room. "He's following up on a lead."

"On his own?"

"No," Morgan shot back in a hurry. "Definitely not. He's with me while I go through forensics. He's just… into it. You know?"

"I'd like to—"

"Agent Dunleavy!" Morgan cringed at Howie's shout echoing through the room. He rushed toward her, clearly excited.

"We've got it!"

Morgan slammed her hand over the speaker to the phone, though a bit too late. Metcalf yelled into her ear, "Who was that, Morgan? What is—?"

"Gotta go, Director," Morgan said. She held the phone out. "Update you soon!"

She ended the call and a deep breath escaped her. When the app minimized on the display she quickly turned the device off. She didn't need any more near-misses with Metcalf. She only had one concern at the moment.

"Is it done?" she asked the jubilant Howie.

"We've got it," he confirmed, practically bouncing in his step.

"Where?"

"Clev…"

Clev shook his head. "Ward has it."

"I do," Ward replied, fixing his thick frames to his face with a single finger. "Here."

He extended his hand, and Morgan saw that a syringe rested along his palm. The slender tube was filled with the compound. They had discussed it without ever actually mentioning the name—afraid their musings might tumble in the wrong direction. But it had to be right; it had to be what they needed. There wasn't time for second-guessing anymore. Everything, all hope of ending the nightmare, lay in the syringe and its contents.

Acetylcholine.

"This will—?"

"It isn't a cure," Ward said.

Clev jumped in. "And no, we aren't positive it will have the effect you're hoping for. The injection he's received might have permanently damaged that area of the brain."

Acetylcholine was the only neurotransmitter missing from the equation to course-correct the brain back to reason from the unending rage. If she could reason with Ben, if only for a minute, she might have a chance to truly reach him. To pull him back.

She held tight to the syringe like a lifeline. "It's the only play we've got."

Ward kept close. "Just know that a shock like this could do more harm than good."

Morgan nodded. "I know. I got it."

"Do you need…" The question from Howie faded, all three

nervous for the answer.

"You've done enough. More than enough," she said, tucking the syringe in her breast pocket. She smiled to them all in turn, each one blushing slightly from the praise. "Thank you, but I have to finish this myself."

She gathered up the files procured from the medical examiner's office. Tackling Ben alone wasn't the best of plans. Having backup would be the smart move. However, with a citywide manhunt going on for Thirteen, having the Clevingers with her would be a liability. It had to be her and her alone.

Now all I have to do is find Ben before it's too late.

CHAPTER TWENTY-FOUR

Metcalf heard the click on the other end of the line. Morgan had left her hanging. Not only that, but she was holding back pertinent information and working with an unknown third party without authorization. Morgan had failed to pass along a single useful update to Metcalf or the operations team since she departed. Metcalf squeezed tight to her cell phone, imagining it belonged to someone's neck—anyone's neck.

The entire situation was unacceptable. She had given the field team a long leash since day one. It signified their prime status in the chain of command. But lately they had been withholding information while in the field. She noticed it during the situation in Chicago with the rogue FBI agent Hendricks. Lincoln had the same issue in Des Moines and was now on the run. Even Riley had gone on his own to investigate the death of Abigail Winslow, rather than notify his colleagues at the DSA for assistance. She demanded updates at all times. Instead, she remained completely clueless.

It matched her feelings toward the current events at the office. Even in the bustling afternoon hours of the work day she stood alone in the main corridor of the DSA warehouse base of operations. She was alone among dozens. The analysts and support staffers scurried on the opposite side of the hall with a quick nod and a quicker pace to be anywhere else. Maybe it had to do with the grimace spread across her face. Or the way she continued to white-knuckle the cell phone, suffocating the life from the cold plastic. It didn't matter. Her actions, her point of pride at her position, and her need for control over every aspect of the day-to-day operations left her without any at all.

Down the hall Sullivan met with Zac. The deputy director's eyes were black holes, swallowing all light from overhead. His shoulders slumped forward, and the amount of weight he passed off to Zac as he hugged the tech close to chat made it appear the man was dead on his feet.

Concern remained for Metcalf. Despite his look and his age, she worried over a failure to anticipate his next move. She had failed to glean the slightest detail of what was to come.

A number of breaches in security continued to crop up, most emanating from Zac's terminal. Part of her wished that someone else had simply accessed their sensitive files and used the trusting tech as a patsy. The truth, however, was obvious and had been for some time, ever since she had driven him away by maintaining a shroud of secrecy. From her vantage, Zac and Sullivan's conversation appeared innocuous enough; it was a gentle debate over the incoming and outgoing reports held tight by the young tech. Why did she think it was anything more?

Because with Sullivan *everything* was more. Everything became part of something larger. She had learned that the hard way with Ben's so-called assessment hearing; the meeting had been little more than an attempt to subvert her latest recruit. Her concern over Ben's loyalty was primary in her thoughts, and she had a certain reticence at speaking to the man for fear of what was being relayed. Now, with the team out of reach, her trepidation returned to his safety.

Metcalf started for her office. Heels clacked loudly, a bullet train warning everyone in her path to step aside. She refused to make eye contact with a group of departing researchers, though she took note of their questioning stares in her periphery. She had never attempted to connect more with any of her subordinates. It was another in a long line of regrets.

As she stepped into the formal waiting area outside her office, her rapid approach stirred Stephanie Atwater from her computer screen. "Director? Is everything—?"

"Office," Metcalf replied without stopping. She opened the door and was inside before the edict completed. "Now."

Stephanie sidestepped the returning door, and she slipped into the office before letting it collapse into the frame with a loud crash. Metcalf noted her arrival, double checked their privacy, then continued to the far end of the room.

"Can I get you...?" Stephanie paused, the question lost to the buzzing of Metcalf's phone. The director glanced down. The message ran along the screen.

It's done. You sure letting her go was the right move?

Fingers danced along the keyboard. *Did I have another choice?*

No, she would have fought tooth and nail.

I figured. Monitor her movements. We'll bring her in when the time is right.

Seconds passed, and each delay troubled her. She held her breath, waiting for the reply. Her heart beat once more when the phone chirped an answer.

Confirmed. Good luck, Susan.

She deleted the conversation with a swipe of her finger and tucked the device away. Metcalf replayed the news over in her mind. *It's done.* It was one more detail she had managed to secure. One more contingency was now in place. None of that made her feel any more prepared than a moment earlier. There was still too much that could go wrong; there were too many ways to lose.

"Susan?" Stephanie asked again. She hovered near the door.

Metcalf failed to hear her, or the growing concern in her voice. Having one more contingency in place failed to ease her troubled thoughts. Precious seconds continued to slip away from her.

At the back of the office Metcalf opened her closet. Her suitcase rested on the bottom shelf next to a pair of heels and sneakers. The black nylon hit the tile floor with a thud. Her fingers worked the zipper with ease until the bag lay open along the floor. Reaching within, she withdrew a smaller bag tucked into the side of the suitcase. It was a similar black and blended into the material of the larger travel bag.

"I need twenty-four hours." Metcalf swung the go-bag over to her desk. After pulling open the zipper she found a number of IDs, passports, cash, and clothes. Underneath a pair of black pants lay a Sig Sauer 1911 Fastback. She hadn't laid eyes on the sleek firearm in a long time. She buried it, then peered back to the waiting and concerned personal assistant. "I'm in meetings. Conferences. Personal crap. I don't care what you come up with. Just sell it."

"For Sullivan?" Stephanie asked in a quiet voice. Even in the privacy of the office he was mentioned only in a whisper. The fact unnerved both of them. It reminded Metcalf of her counter-measures and how quickly she had been to put them in place. A small pen-shaped device fell from her top drawer and she set it along the tabletop. The red light upon the mechanism blinked rapidly for three seconds, then fell black. The sweep completed, and all listening devices in the area were neutralized.

"For everyone," Metcalf snapped, shutting the bag and sling-ing over her shoulder. Her eyes fell slightly, and a soft breath escaped her. "But yes."

Stephanie nodded at the admission. Metcalf appreciated her silence on the subject. The director was disliked and avoided by choice when it came to the majority of the staff. That wasn't the case with the blond-haired bombshell in the knee-high boots. She chose her boss over all others.

"He was talking to Zac," Stephanie noted.

Metcalf let the duffel settle next to her desk for a moment. From her bottom-right drawer she produced a small key ring. She shuffled through the varied keys until the right one came into view. Metcalf walked slowly to the credenza in the corner. She removed the water pitcher, the cold pot of coffee, and the tablecloth beneath to reveal a hidden compartment. After she placed the key within, the lock clicked soundly and the doors slid in both directions. Metcalf procured a small box from within the hidden space. Returning to the center of the room, she placed it in the side pocket of her bag. She stopped short of her curious companion, a hand coming to rest on the young woman's shoul-der.

"Steph," Metcalf said with concern. "Keep your eyes on them and your ears open."

"Always." Metcalf retrieved her bag, then started for the door. The young assistant called her back. "Director? He knows about Des Moines, and about what Lincoln did there. Sullivan's had people watching his apartment. I don't know how long he's known or how he found out, but he—"

"Zac told him," Metcalf answered, her response sullen. Zac's lack of trust in her and her inability to provide any of her own had cemented a bond between the pair conversing in the corri-dor. She deserved his enmity and worked to figure out a way to bring him back to the fold, though she hadn't found success yet.

Each passing day made their relationship that much worse.

"Zac wouldn't, would he?" Worry filled Stephanie's face. Neither of them spoke openly about their previous conversations, yet Bunker Protocol remained at the forefront of every thought that passed between them. It was in every word left unsaid and every question unasked.

"Twenty-four hours," Metcalf nodded to her assistant. "I just need one day, Stephanie."

"How else can I help?"

Metcalf felt her phone in her pocket and the weight of the lock box in her go-bag. There were too many contingencies left on the table. She needed to start closing the gap.

"Book me on a flight to Buffalo. The sooner the better."

CHAPTER TWENTY-FIVE

Her departure stopped Zac mid-sentence. The exact topic eluded him, the conversation varied and menial, even to the detail-oriented Head of Operational Support and Research. They were somewhere between talking about the rapid influx of office supply reorders and an update about the Buffalo operation currently in play when Metcalf left her office.

Not that the occurrence was out of the norm. This, though, appeared different. It was in her rushed steps, and her wearing sneakers instead of the clacking of heels typically noting her presence to the staff. Then there was the bag strapped to her shoulder; it was a black duffel unlike her typical brief bag or suitcase depending on travel arrangements. Everything about her screamed the incongruities of her departure.

Zac could only stare after her in the aftermath. Days passed between their chats now. Metcalf cut him off from internal meetings about policy changes or possible operations. The Buffalo mission was the first time all week she had deigned to schedule time together prior to the briefing. She kept the discussion on the work. She always did, though this again struck him as odd considering their sparse conversations of late.

The lack of trust had come from her. The divide had grown ever since Grissom's death, and it culminated in the lie of Lincoln's double homicide in Des Moines. She had failed to bring Zac in the fold, refused to pass along vital information to win him back — if such a thing was possible. He knew where his loyalty lay: with the man at his side.

Sullivan tsked. The aging deputy director clearly read his companion's thoughts in the silence of the moment. "More secrets? I was afraid of this."

The concern wasn't misplaced. It rested in his eyes, and in his shaking hands tucked close to the tablet. Why the man had wanted to meet so consistently of late gave the tech pause. There were rules to follow, procedures in place to keep the transparency of their department above board; that was something Metcalf always believed in—or at least she had before the loss of Grissom. Sullivan operated differently, and while it might have struck against the orderly business of the DSA, Zac appreciated playing an integral role again.

Metcalf might not trust him any longer, but Sullivan did. The woman's behavior lately had gone beyond a lack of trust in one man, but in the entire department. Each abuse of power and secret stung him.

Zac closed his eyes and returned to the man at his side. He tried to forget about the departing director as easily as she had them. "What can we do?"

Sullivan smiled. He wrapped his arm around Zac and pulled him close. They started down the hall for his waiting office. "I'm glad to hear you ask that, Zac. I wasn't sure we were on the same page."

"I am," Zac replied. "About the director, anyway."

A nod escaped the deputy director. "Ah. Agent Dunleavy."

"She wouldn't betray the department, sir," Zac said. He recalled the recording of Morgan with Metcalf discussing a cover-up surrounding Lincoln's capture. He had tried to deny it, refused to believe she would knowingly betray him and the DSA. His words weakened with his resolve. "I… I know her, sir."

"She knows you as well," Sullivan said. He stopped before the door and let out a long sigh. "She is a talented operative. She knows how to manipulate you, and she knows how to prey on your doubts and weaknesses. It's a ploy, Zac."

"Why?" Sadness filled the question. There was something more beneath the surface—anger. The same struggle followed him after hearing the recording. He held the same doubts about their one night together, about her true intentions with him. "Why bother with me?"

"You're more important than you know," Sullivan said. "That's why I need you to see the truth. Can I trust you, Zac?"

There was no more time to weigh options, to question his

needs over his wants. It was time to think with his head instead of his heart.

One course remained open for him. He had delayed taking it for so long. He had been lost to Morgan's whispers, her very presence. Evidence mounted against her and Metcalf—evidence that demanded reconciling, not only for his sake but for the DSA. He had spent years building up and maintaining the agency. This was his life's work and he wasn't about to see it thrown away.

A nod escaped him.

"Good," Sullivan said with a grin. "I need your help to find something that's escaped into the world. It is the most vital tool in the history of mankind."

"What?"

Sullivan led the curious tech inside his office and closed the door. "It's called the Wellspring."

CHAPTER TWENTY-SIX

West Potomac Park had always been one of his mother's favorite places. She had taken her two sons to the capital every year for a family vacation. They had always picnicked in the park on the last day of their visit. One spot, in particular, had brought joy to the tired woman. The location was in a grove of Japanese cherry trees overlooking the Tidal Basin and the Washington Monument. Even in the middle of winter when the snow covered the walkways and the white of its banks faded to brown he still found beauty in the space.

Lincoln checked his watch once more. His foot nervously tapped, crunching the remnants of snow surrounding the bench. The sun faded and, with it, the crowds thinned, but the few brave enough to face the elements walked briskly through the area. Lincoln kept his eyes fixed on them while he tried to deflect the nervousness held in his bloodshot orbs with a smile and a nod. He was just a friendly face in the crowd, enjoying the end of a warm spell amid the snow-infected months of the calendar.

It was the exact opposite of his true nature. His nerves were frayed from waiting. He kept reaching for his sidearm to make sure it was still in place.

"Come on." He shifted to find some comfort. His hands squeezed tight to his knees to keep them from shaking. He had arrived earlier than expected. The sun set in the distance, struggling to remain visible for as long as possible. Lincoln stared at the glowing sphere. For over a week he had run fast and hard, trying to figure out his next move. That evening was the first time he found his body stationary, mesmerized by the fading daylight and the rising dark. When he was young he had marveled at the shifting of the day to night—the promise of a new day just over the horizon. It was a certainty to the boy. Now, however, nothing was guaranteed. Not even a new day. Lincoln checked the Timex along his wrist once more. "Where the hell are you?"

"Waiting for someone?"

Lincoln jumped at the voice. He turned to the end of the bench. The man he had awaited sat patiently, as if there the entire time. He smiled, his eyes hidden behind the rounded spectacles on his face. The man known only as the Witness wore the smug look well—and much too often.

"How did you…?" Lincoln tried to ask, looking beyond the bench for some trail left of his arrival. There should have been footprints in the snow, some indication of the man's path he had somehow missed during his distracted thoughts. He found none.

"You said seven," the Witness confirmed. The gold band of his timepiece glinted against the light of the lamp post overhead. "It is now seven. Worried, Agent MacKenzie?"

Lincoln's head lowered as he searched the area. A young couple hugged close as they passed. They failed to notice the pair. He shuffled closer to the Witness, his voice barely a whisper. "You know I am."

"Relax," the Witness said with a smirk. The glow behind his lenses was muted, but the angle of the man's position on the bench gave Lincoln a clear view of scars over the Witness' eyes. Deep scars. Catching the stare, the man in black shifted to face his companion, causing his opaque lenses to reflect an orange hue from the nearby lamp post. The Witness pulled his black trench coat tighter. "We're simply two people braving the elements same as everyone else. Though not for long, I hope."

"Yeah," Lincoln said. "I'd hate for you to catch something."

"I would thank you for your consideration, if you actually cared."

"I called."

"You had to," the Witness said. "Agent Dunleavy?"

Lincoln's gaze fell to the snow. Of course he knew. The Witness had anticipated that Lincoln would reach out to Morgan. He wrote as much on a note card left in the aftermath of their meeting at the Savery. Morgan had been Lincoln's one true friend at the DSA—the one person capable of viewing the world through the same lens as him. They had gone through similar trials and survived similar failures. The arrogant son of a bitch had warned Lincoln not to pursue her assistance. The stubborn agent had refused to listen, believing in his friend and colleague more than the enigmatic man with the scarred eyes.

He was wrong.

"She didn't want to hear it. Just like you thought."

"Knew," the Witness corrected with the wag of his finger. Lincoln wanted to snatch the digit and break it with a single motion, but held fast.

"How?" he asked through gritted teeth.

The Witness tapped his glasses. "Simple observation, Lincoln. But that's not why we're here, is it?"

"No," Lincoln muttered. His head was low, submissive to his companion. "It isn't."

"You have rethought my request for assistance?"

The snow crunched hard under Lincoln's heel. "You mean betraying the DSA?"

"You wouldn't be betraying anything," the Witness replied. His voice was calm and confident. It never wavered, unlike Lincoln's. "You would be saving your former colleagues."

"You make it sound so clear cut."

"It is."

The snappy responses from the Witness burned through Lincoln. His anger rose, and his chest heaved. For as long as he could remember he had fought for something: an ideal. He had always pursued some lofty goal, be it freedom, his country, or the notion of protecting others incapable of doing so on their own. Through it all, either with the Army, the Secret Service, or the DSA, he had always believed the good being done outweighed the bad. There were compromises, small measures lost in the shades of gray, but they were for the greater good.

Or so he had thought.

Had he been wrong about everything? Every word spoken by the tall, thin twig of a man beside him gave him more reason to doubt.

"I understand your reticence," the Witness said, reading Lincoln's tortured face.

Lincoln pushed off the bench and stepped closer to the walkway. Exhausted eyes pleaded with the man resting comfortably against the cold seat. "Give me something. Anything. You talk about these things, the DSA, this whatever the hell you call it, the Wellspring, but everything around you is left in vague overtones."

"You require specifics."

"Yes!" Lincoln shouted, the affirmation echoing through the trees and into the night sky.

"Very well," the Witness said. He stood, looking toward the bright lights surrounding the Washington Monument in the distance. "In five days the DSA will fall. There will be a coup, and with it everything I am working toward will be put in jeopardy."

Lincoln laughed at the impossibility of the Witness' story. The man had described it so clearly and succinctly one could almost believe it had already happened. It was like he had read the events in the paper and was summarizing the entire affair. The Witness remained standing, refusing to acknowledge Lincoln's reaction.

"That'll never happen," Lincoln said.

"Sit down, Lincoln," the Witness said, pointing to the bench. He greeted a new pair of pedestrians with a warm smile. After they had passed, his hand showcased the seat. Lincoln, his laughter all but spent, reluctantly obliged. "You asked for this. You wanted to know details, and I have given them. Your department is already broken, and the loyalties between Metcalf and Sullivan have been shattered. When the coup ends, the DSA in its new form will take up only one task: the Wellspring."

"Let's say I buy into this," Lincoln said, leaning forward on the cold bench. "How is finding this Wellspring a bad thing?"

"Think of a nuclear weapon in the hands of a Middle-Eastern nation."

"Not dramatic at all."

"It will make the DSA too powerful. They will seek more. Opening the secrets of the Wellspring cannot happen, Lincoln. We have traveled too far down that road already and I have seen its end. Once the DSA, once Gregory Sullivan, opens that box there is no coming back."

The box. Lincoln remembered old stories his mother had shared before he went to bed each night. Myths and legends from across the world dating back centuries. "You're talking Pandora's Box?"

"Worse," the Witness answered, staring the confused agent down.

"Yet you want it for yourself."

The Witness paused before answering. "To destroy it."

"Don't lie now, Witness," Lincoln said.

"I haven't," he said. "I wouldn't. Not to you, Lincoln. But time is working against us. I need your help."

"Against my own people."

The Witness' hand fell on his shoulder and squeezed. "*They* are the enemy, Lincoln. They have to be stopped."

The words burrowed deep into his thundering chest. They took root and festered, infecting him. Each rang true — truer than he cared to admit. There was something wrong with the DSA.

Lincoln nodded, his silent affirmation solidifying their new arrangement.

The two men left the cold of the bench behind and stepped on the walkway. They headed toward the lights of the city. Their talk continued, sparse yet determined, all pointing toward a plan in the making. They prepared for a new operation.

They had to stop the DSA before it was too late.

CHAPTER TWENTY-SEVEN

Two hours remained.

The deadline loomed. It occupied Morgan's every thought. Her search to find her dying partner had been a failure on every level, and left Morgan without a shred of hope. Hours had been spent circling associates of Horace Waters, tracking down Ben's old address and a dozen other hotspots. Unfortunately, she didn't know enough, never cared to know enough about Ben. Her distance had condemned them both to this situation. If she had pushed for more, been better about understanding him on any personal level, she would have found him. She *had* to find him. She was the only one left to help save him. She was the only chance in hell Ben had at seeing another sunrise.

If he could be saved.

Believing she was already too late was a distinct possibility and one she immediately put away. Her key slid in the lock of the motel room. Her fingers nudged the crust glued to the inside of her eyelids as she attempted to clear away two days' worth of cobwebs and insomniac tendencies. She wanted to rest. Her body demanded it. More than that, she wanted a hot bath in a Jacuzzi tub with room service and chocolate-covered strawberries for dessert. She wanted anything but to still be in Buffalo, frozen to the core, hunting for her partner before he killed someone.

A shower would suffice. Five minutes of peace to battle back the fear, the doubt, everything she had powered through with the Clevingers.

The syringe remained tucked safely in her breast pocket. What the vial amounted to was an overdose of reason. Acetylcholine. She had no idea if it would work. No one did. However, the syringe remained her only option. The clock continued to tick by, second by second, bringing Ben's life closer and closer to the end.

It was time to call in the cavalry, Metcalf's holier-than-thou attitude be damned, though she was the last person Morgan wanted to contact. Their superior would be furious at their situation and how it had come to be. Morgan didn't care. After her five-minute shower her next move was a call to Baxter for help, even if it meant the end of her partnership with Ben. If he was found out, there would be no avoiding the jail sentence the DSA had saved him from. It was better to be alive in a cell, though, than dead after committing the worst sin known to man.

Had she been thinking, if her eyes were on the room around her she would have noticed the differences immediately—the destruction throughout. The bed frame laid upended along the right-hand wall; the mattress was askew at the base of the opposite wall. Glass was scattered along the carpet. Bottles. Light fixtures. Everything in the room had been shattered to pieces.

If her thoughts had been on the present instead of the possible futures heading toward her, she would have heard the creaking floorboard behind the door when she closed it. She also would have heard the labored breath of the man waiting for her.

"Hey, Morgan," a deep voice called out.

Morgan jumped, waking to the room for the first time. The devastation. The lack of light, the non-functional switch, and the other presence in the room. "What the—?"

A hand caught her wrist and shoved her deeper into the room. Even before he stepped out of the shadows she knew who it was, who it had to be. All her searching had amounted to nothing. All the time wasted, all the fear at the ticking clock—constantly spinning out of her control—all to save one man's life had met with failure. He had been waiting for her the entire time.

Ben sneered. Strips of moonlight snuck through the torn curtain over the window, beaming off the whites of his teeth. His wide eyes burned red from his sandy pupils. They grew with each step toward her.

"How's the head?"

CHAPTER TWENTY-EIGHT

Since their first meeting, Morgan had found her partner sarcastic, witty, and less than charming in most circumstances. Above all, though, he was compassionate. For the work and those involved, and for the victims especially, Ben threw everything he had into doing the right thing. Morgan had stood by his side proudly, though she had failed to verbalize that in any fashion, preferring to drive a wedge between them rather than bond.

She held back her feelings toward the man she had tried to save for the last day not out of some deep-seated admiration of the man. No, it was more than that. She held back because she never wanted him to change. Recognition of the good in people had the tendency to change them. Ego won out over all in her eyes, her view of the world. But to her, Ben was a decent man. Standing in the darkness of the less-than-accommodating motel room just outside the city limits, Morgan experienced something new in his presence.

Fear.

Ben was gone; he had been lost to the infection flooding his system. It was in his stance, the look in his eyes, and even the corner of his bottom lip creasing his cheek like a scar running up the side of his face.

"Ben," she said. Her feet shuffled back for the door as she worked her way through the furniture strewn throughout the room. "You have to listen."

"No," his voice boomed.

His fist came out of nowhere. It jumped from the shadows and collided with her cheek. The blow drove her toward a nearby dresser and the shattered screen of the small television. She crashed hard into her wounded shoulder. She refused to cry out, though her eyes watered from the pain.

Morgan hoped against all reason to talk Ben down from his mounting anger, the growing rage coursing through his veins in the form of a medicinal cocktail developed by a warped version of a deranged scientist. Hope left her in the form of a long stream of blood spat on the broken television. Her cheek refilled with the warm liquid immediately. She struggled to her knees. Her right hand reassured her of the syringe still in place in her breast pocket. She just needed an opening.

She turned, Ben looming over her. "Dammit, Ben. This thing inside you is going to kill you. I can help."

He lifted her up with ease and tossed her across the room into the bed. More pain pulsed through her back and down her legs. The bed frame gave her little cushioning, and kept her somewhat upright.

"You *are* helping, Morgan," Ben fumed, his words foaming at the mouth. "Now shut up."

"Listen!"

"No!" The fist slammed into her ribs, and a second hook connected firmly with her right temple. She fell hard, and the breath was ripped from her lungs. The shadow of her partner stole the light from the room. "I am tired of your lies. The DSA, you and Metcalf, stole my life and I want to know why. Tell me the truth!"

The Ruger glinted in the moonlight. Blood dripped from her lip, and her eyes were stuck on the barrel of the gun. She coughed hard, splattering crimson along the carpet in a shallow pool. She swiped at her bruised face, clearing her field of vision as she faced the armed man above her. She refused to blink, refused to beg. Cool eyes met her attacker.

"Do it, Ben," Morgan said. "If that's what you need. You go ahead and do it."

His hands shook in anger. "Tell me why you did this to me!"

The metal pressed against her forehead. The cold comforted her for the first time. She grabbed the barrel and held it tight to her skin.

"No."

Ben screamed at her defiance. Morgan seized the opportunity. She drove her body up hard at her partner. He tried to shift the gun back to her but he was too late. She caught his arm and used his momentum to flip him over her shoulder into the wall beside them.

By the time the syringe was in her hand, Ben was up and racing toward her. The attack had only increased his rage. It made him sloppy, just as she had predicted. His control was gone. It had slowly deteriorated ever since his injection by the twisted clone of Howard Clevinger. His arm shot out, skirting above her shoulder as she sidestepped the assault. The motion carried him past her. In a split second her hand rose over her head and drove down hard. The needle pierced Ben's neck, and her thumb slammed down on the plunger. Ben's left arm shot around, the back of his fist catching her along her wounded ribs, and she fell once more. Ben removed the syringe, staring at it with crazed eyes.

"You bitch!" he screamed. "What did you do?"

"Don't fight it," she muttered. Each word drove hot pokers through her chest. A broken rib, she thought. Definitely something out of place. All of it was worth it to give him a chance to find a way out of his anger, a dim hope against his dark impulse. "Listen to me, Ben. You have to—"

Ben fell to his knees and shrieked in pain. His hands collapsed against his chest, and he spun away from her. There was a chance, a very likely chance that the neurotransmitter might have a negative reaction with the infected. She found her feet, fighting to stay upright, and dragged her wounded frame across the room to her flailing partner.

"Come on, Ben." Her hand reached out for him, and she held the other tight against her ribs. "Come back to me. Come—"

She noticed the gun too late. By the time she spotted it, the screaming had vanished like a turned switch. He had played her as easily as she did him mere moments ago; her guard was down. The butt of the Ruger arced back from his right hand and connected with her chin soundly. The force took her off her feet, and her body suspended in the air for a brief second before crashing to the carpet in a heap.

Dazed, Morgan fought to refocus. The room spun. Dark spots filled her vision.

"You're going to wish for that bullet, Morgan."

Morgan tried to lift her head, only to fall flat to the ground.

Her vision faded to darkness. Ben's hand reached out for her, his words carrying her toward the thick black of night.

"That's the truth."

CHAPTER TWENTY-NINE

She thought of Zac first. Morgan didn't know why her thoughts turned to him. She specifically thought of their morning together when he made her breakfast, touting the world's best omelet was on its way. He delivered on breakfast and more. So did she.

It had been a beautiful morning.

This was something different. The tranquility of the past, her time with the man she shared a bed with, faded away to the shadowed motel room. Her groaning awoke more than her senses; it snapped her back to the physical agony of the last few hours and the torment at the hands of the man she called partner. Ben held tight to the Ruger hovering in front of her face.

"Ben, please..." she said. She pushed through his ramblings; she tried to force him to peer at her in an effort to suppress the screams of conspiracy and betrayal for only an instant. Ben believed she had ruined his life, that she and Metcalf and the rest of the DSA had plotted with Horace Waters.

She tried to reason with him, to ply for time. Her hands had been tied haphazardly behind her—a hurried attempt to restrain her. Morgan wondered how much time had been lost, time she did not have in abundance if the Clevingers' prognosis of the situation was to be trusted. The sloppy job on her makeshift cuffs and the agony of her wounds indicated no more than a few minutes had passed. Time remained, but as the pistol inched closer and the crazed eyes of her partner bored down on her she wondered if it would be enough.

Her concern wasn't for Ben anymore. The acetylcholine cocktail was in place and doing everything possible to combat his illness. He would either survive the effects of the virus or he wouldn't at this point. No, any time gained with her pleas was for her own life.

The hammer cocked on the gun, and the click echoed in her mind. Morgan closed her eyes. Her fingers fought for freedom from the zip ties locking her in place.

"...you will, Morgan," she heard him say, though she was unsure what injustice she was being accused of this time. "You will."

The gun went off, a brilliant flash of white filling her eyes. Then darkness returned.

"Dammit, Ben!" There was a hole in the wall beside her head — inches from her face.

Ben grinned fiendishly. The gun returned to her forehead, a small sliver of heat escaping the barrel. "Last chance! The truth. Why did the DSA ruin my life? Why did they take everything from me? Where is Emily Wright?"

It clicked in that moment. *Emily Wright.* Not the name itself, but the way he said it. It was the fact that he even mentioned her at all. The entire time, ever since his run-in with the evil version of Howard Clevinger — a statement she still had trouble reconciling in her mind — Ben had focused on one person: himself. Every conspiracy led to him. Every web of lies, every secret, held before him centered solely on screwing him over and no one else. It was all about Ben.

Until now.

In her hesitation to respond, buying for more time, she saw Ben again. His eyes were no longer lost to a hazy, bloodshot red. Sweat dried along his brow, and his hands stopped shaking. He was being sewn together, stitched back into place by the cocktail.

Just not fast enough.

"Ben..." Morgan started. She tugged lightly to release her hands, and the right slipped through the haphazard restraint. "I don't—"

"Don't lie to me! Where is she?"

She locked eyes with him. "Who is she, Ben? Who is Emily Wright?"

"You know who she is!" he screamed, his voice cracking at each word. "My partner! My friend!"

"*I'm* your partner, Ben," Morgan replied. She held his glare, kept him locked on her. "Look at me. Just look at me, Ben. You wanted an inch of trust and I fought it as much as I could, but you kept earning it. I'm your partner, Ben. Remember that."

Her left hand slipped loose, but she tucked it close. Ben's eyes fluttered. His arm struggled to stay locked on her with the Ruger.

"Come on," she muttered. "You remember that, don't you?"

He shook his head, and his hand collapsed against his temple. "That's another lie, isn't it? Another damn lie. You…"

Ben stumbled, and he dropped the sidearm to the floor of the motel room. Now empty, his hand joined his left at his temples.

"Let it happen, Ben."

His eyes widened, catching sight of the empty syringe in the corner of the room. "You did this to me. You—"

He leapt at her, one final scream escaping his lips. It was one final, desperate attempt to finalize Thirteen's plan for him—to turn him into a killer.

As he leapt, hands out in front of him, she found her opening. Launching herself from the chair, Morgan led with her forehead and caught Ben's chin solidly. His body was driven up and back by the blow. He landed hard on the ground amid the shattered glass from the light fixtures.

"How did…?" he struggled to ask, his question calm and melodic compared to the grit of earlier. He looked up at Morgan, eyes white and serene as if waking from a dream.

Morgan refused to take a chance. Her foot swung hard, connecting with his cheek. His head snapped hard to the left. His body collapsed as sleep finally took hold. Morgan huffed, letting cold air fill her lungs. It was agony on her ribs, but she allowed herself a thin smile.

"You'll thank me for this someday," she said to her unconscious partner. "Trust me."

CHAPTER THIRTY

His mouth tasted like cotton balls. That was Ben's first sensation upon waking from a deep slumber. The second was the odor: pungent and acrid—dirt combined with sweat and grime. Then he realized it came from him. His eyes snapped open, expecting the sound of beeping and buzzing from various hospital instruments to fill his ears and the antiseptic smell to replace the filth he must have accumulated over the course of days.

Instead, he woke to the darkness of his motel room. His bag sat where he had left it near the bathroom at the back. The channel guide rested on the nightstand within reach, though he hadn't had the chance to use the television. Ben tried to sit up, but the pain instantly jolted down his right side and across his forehead. He settled back into the pillows. He scanned the room, until his gaze fell on the shadow at the side of the bed.

Morgan finished taping up her naked midsection. Her movements mesmerized her waking partner. The medicinal tape wrapped under her chest and around her abs in a tight formation to keep everything in place. Ben noticed bruises on the outskirts of the bandage. They were purple and deep blue, and they also ran down her arm, beneath her eyes, and above a cut on her lip. Morgan winced with each rotation of the tape until it came to an end. She tucked the end tight to her side, then reached for a black t-shirt—one of his—and slipped it over her head with care.

"Hey," Ben muttered, his voice cracked and torn. He shifted higher on the stack of pillows around his head. The effort caused him to cringe and cough. "Oh, that hurts."

"I would imagine," she said. She pulled her long curls away

from her face. She shifted beside him, then rested uncomfortably in a nearby chair. For as much as every movement caused him immense pain, Morgan appeared much worse off. Agony strained her deep brown irises.

"What the hell did they put in my drink? I swear, the next bar you pick—"

"You picked it, Ben." She smirked through swollen lips. The grin fell away and she sucked air carefully, leaning forward. Sadness rested in her eyes. "That was two days ago."

"What?" Ben sat up, the attempt weak, and he fell back in defeat at the sudden movement. "How is that possible?"

"You don't remember anything?"

"You bailed, and I…" He grazed his cheek, where a large lump was swelling up. His fingers reeled back, the merest touch excruciating. "What the hell?"

"Sorry," Morgan said. She kept a hand on her left side. Her eyes closed with each shift of her weight on the chair. "I figured hospitals weren't a safe bet. Besides, I'm kind of sick of them."

They couldn't take the chance of him being recognized. How he came to be in this state, though, continued to elude him. He also wasn't sure of the extent of his injuries—unseen in the dim light afforded by the closed curtains.

"How bad?"

"You have multiple contusions. Dehydration. There's lots of bruising, but nothing much beneath the surface." Her swollen eyes ran over him like he was a medical chart. "You're definitely not looking one hundred percent."

"You?"

"Some of it," she said, the corner of her lip perking with pride.

"Great." Two days since the bar. He lost two days somehow. What had happened? Morgan left. She had been angry, and rightfully so. He had wanted to follow, to apologize. Instead, he had stayed to pay the check. And after? He circled to the same question.

"How bad, Morgan?" Her sad eyes fell away. "Tell me."

"You didn't know what you were doing," she said, her words barely a whisper.

It snapped loose. The floodgates opened, exploding into view. Ben fell deeper into the pillow, staring at the ceiling of the motel room like it was an elaborate canvas as the missing events tumbled out of him; a slideshow on the cracked, white paint.

"Clevinger," he uttered. Wide eyes suddenly aware greeted his partner. "He came out of nowhere. Howard Clevinger. He did this to me, didn't he?"

Morgan nodded. "He was busing tables at the bar. Looking for subjects, I guess."

"He was behind it all." The answer fell out of him as he finally pieced together the missing puzzle of the last two days. The injections. The science behind the virus was completely original from Bellbrook, yet it had garnered similar results in the undertaking — more loss of life. "How? I thought Lincoln —"

"He did," Morgan stopped him. They fell silent at the sound of sirens echoing through the streets outside.

"We need to move. Baxter might..." Ben struggled to sit up.

Morgan forced him down with a light touch along his arm. "We're safe here. I called Baxter. Took some explaining, but he's not pursuing you for anything. He's out looking for *him*."

"Clevinger."

"But not." Ben shot her a look. She rolled her eyes. "I can't believe I'm saying this, but... it was another Clevinger."

"What?"

Morgan shrugged. "Clone."

"Stop," Ben replied, waiting for the punch line. Her face stayed stone cold. "Seriously?"

"Yup," Morgan said. She leaned against the back of the chair. "I met three others."

Three others? Ben couldn't believe she had managed to say it with a straight face. Clones. Multiple versions of Clevinger. "That's disturbing on so many levels."

"You're telling me. Still, they saved your life. If they hadn't shown up when they did and helped me figure this out..."

"Morgan," Ben called, reaching for her. She kept her distance, unable to look in his direction.

As each waking moment passed he witnessed more of the missing time, unfolding as if the lock had been picked on his short-term memory and now flooded his senses. The rage, the unreasonably fulfilling rage he embodied from Clevinger's experiment. Horace Waters. Jamar Price. Everything. None of the memories affected him like the pain he had inflicted on Morgan—and the reason he did so. He reached for her again and she flinched back. He had earned the reaction, though it tore his heart out.

"I said it was all right, Riley."

"You did," Ben said. He refused to let the pain win, and he managed to sit up to face his partner. Morgan tried to intercede, but held back at his wave. "I'm talking about before. At the bar? I shouldn't have said anything about Zac like that. It wasn't my place and never will be."

Morgan's lip curled; her hand was slow to fall on his. "Everyone gets one rage virus excuse." She patted his cracked knuckles. After standing, she started for the door. "You need to get some rest. We're paid up for a few more days. I owed the clerk anyway."

"Why?"

"Doesn't matter." Her eyes were at the front window overlooking the expressway in the distance and the lightening horizon.

"Morgan?" he asked, lying back on the lumpy mattress. She turned at the sound of his pain. "Modine? Really?"

"Riley." Her thin glare cut through the room.

Ben threw up his hands. "Has he shown you his comic book collection?"

"Riley!"

"Just saying," he replied with a laugh. "Mine's bigger."

Morgan joined him in forgetting their shared pain. "You're lucky I know you're actually talking about comics."

The sun cracked the horizon behind Morgan and the opened door. A thin coating of snow had fallen through the night. Ben had forgotten how much he loved the snow in the morning light. He didn't realize how much he truly missed his home.

His smile faded as curiosity took over. "Why?"

Morgan's brow furrowed. "You know exactly—"

"Not about Zac, sorry," he continued. His hand clutched his forehead as if he was attempting to hold on to his lingering thought. "Must be the drugs in my system. I'm bouncing around like an idiot. What I meant was, why did Clevinger do this here and now?"

Morgan shrugged. "Maybe it was meant to be another experiment?"

"Why, though?" It was the timing of the affair from start to finish that bothered Ben. Every detail ran through his thoughts at a blistering speed, yet nothing added up. "Just to draw us out? To bring the DSA here?"

"Oh, hell."

"Morgan?" His partner's cheeks sagged, and the shadows swallowed all light from her eyes. She rushed to the corner of the room, a pained look trailing her every move. She wrapped her black peacoat tight around her. Checking her hip holster, she confirmed the presence of her Glock. "What is it?"

"No." She pulled her keys free from her pocket. "It wasn't to draw us out. Dammit. It had nothing to do with the DSA or any of the innocent people caught up in his madness. Not a damn thing. Ben, I have to—"

"Go," he said, recognizing her urgency.

"Are you—?"

"Go, Morgan. Hurry."

The door slammed shut behind her without another word. The car screeched through the parking lot toward the street. Ben found what comfort he could on the bed. Wrapped in the darkness of the room, he wondered if they would ever be in time to save the day, or if they were doomed to always be too little, too late.

Ben closed his eyes, afraid of the answer.

CHAPTER THIRTY-ONE

She was too late. Even as she slammed on the brakes and left the rental car double-parked in the middle of the bustling downtown street, she couldn't shake the sensation. She had blown through every red light, ignored every stop sign. She hadn't been fast enough, hadn't been familiar enough with her surroundings to make better time, if such a thing was possible. Hours had passed since she had heard from them. She had spent the entire evening hunting her partner—only to ignore the true threat.

When she noticed the door to the ramshackle tenement was ajar her worst fears spilled out. She ran from the sedan, hand to her ribs—the pain screaming worse than her thoughts. The door slammed against the peeling paint. Dust circled the air from the impact, though she was already halfway down the hall and too focused on what lay ahead to care about any damage caused to the apartment.

"Clevingers!" she yelled, entering the wide expanse where they stored their equipment. Beakers and centrifuges lay shattered along the floor. Shards of glass crunched under her heel. "Dammit. Whatever you call yourselves, just ans—"

She stopped in mid-step. Throughout the drive, throughout the panic, she had held to a small sliver of hope that she was wrong. But the vacant stare of Howie's eyes told the truth. She had been right all along.

All three lay crumpled in the center of the room, reaching for each other in the end. Blood was spattered on their clothes, from the *Tragically Hip* shirt of Clev to the speckled bowtie of Howie and the rectangular glasses of Ward. Stab wounds marked their flesh. There were shallow cuts along their appendages and deeper ones along their torsos. They had known pain in the end. They had suffered for the life they saved.

"No," Morgan whispered. She had let this happen. The three clones of Howard Clevinger were dead because she had failed to see the true threat, to understand that throughout their search for a cure, the man known as Thirteen had performed his own search. He had found them and she hadn't been around to help when they needed her.

She had let them down.

Morgan sank to her knees, eyes washing over the men that had put themselves at risk for her. Did they know? Were they aware that while they had been hunting their brother for his acts, he had been hunting them? She hated her ignorance. Ben's fate clouded her judgment. It had been her only priority. She should have seen this; she should have suspected it on some level. Clevingers were not to be underestimated.

She stopped, breath catching in her throat at the sight of the far wall. Three words were written using the blood of the three victims tossed in the center of the room like a pile of garbage in a refuse dump.

NOT HOWARD CLEVINGER

In just over two weeks' time Thirteen had taken more than a dozen lives. At the moment Morgan only cared about the three at her feet. Their deaths demanded justice.

She damn well was going to get it for them. The clone of Howard Clevinger numbered Thirteen was going to pay for everything he had done. It was the only promise left to give the dead men at her feet. Her promise was the only thing she could offer them in the silence of their deaths. And she swore to keep it, no matter how long it took.

CHAPTER THIRTY-TWO

The steady tap of his finger along the edge of his desk provided a circadian rhythm to Sullivan's ceaseless pondering. It was time, finally and absolutely. It was time to make his move, time to push ahead, and time to change the course of history.

They were lofty ambitions, but those were always his to wield. From his beginnings in politics, Sullivan had measured success by a growing legacy which could never be denied by the future. His was negligible. Mistakes of his youth had countered the message promoted to his constituents, and his time in office had been cut short by the never-ending news cycle and snippets of unnamed sources able to recall more about the incidents in question than he could despite his so-called involvement in them.

That was the country on the surface. What Sullivan proclaimed, what he strove for in the intervening years while begging for scraps from rich donors and clandestine organizations, was to show what lay beneath. The true destiny of America. Hell, the true path of the *world* should they choose to align their ideals.

The Wellspring was in the open at last. It was out of reach from the major players in the drama, able to be snatched up and claimed should the right person pursue such noble means. And Greg Sullivan was nothing if not known for his nobility.

He stared at the computer monitor, the only light present in the room. A camera feed of Operations ran across the entire screen, displaying Zac hunched over his keyboard. He clacked away in silence as he picked away at the code obscuring Metcalf's files—the final safety measure hoarding her secrets.

Sullivan would have them all. Zac was a means to an end, but a loyal one. He saw the world the same as Sullivan. Metcalf's agenda clouded the true good the DSA was able to accomplish.

His phone rang. Sullivan's tapping ended at the sudden chime. His exhaustion played with his field of vision and he failed to identify the number on the display. Fingers ran deep along his eyelids in an attempt to bury his weariness.

"Yes?"

"Riley is on the move," the voice replied. With the cold wind slamming along the receiver, Sullivan caught little more than the man's sharp tone.

"He survived?" Riley was nothing if not proficient at evading death. He had managed it in Bellbrook, where thousands had fallen. He did the same in Chicago during the Promethean debacle. Luck had had his back on that one. And now? Victims in the double digits, yet Riley managed to walk away. "Remarkable."

"He's a little weathered from the affair, but he's still breathing," the man said. A loud click rang out, the chambering of a round in a high-powered rifle. "For the moment."

"I..." Sullivan hesitated. His orders had been clear: contain the situation in Buffalo and remove all evidence of the group's presence. Horace Waters was dead, and the main impediment to their secrecy had been secured. Riley and his unending questions were another matter, one that could be silenced with a single bullet.

"Sullivan? Are we a go?"

Metcalf had recruited the newcomer for a reason. She had tracked his movements for years, maneuvered events to include him on her paltry field team. There had to be a reason, one he failed to pry loose — another secret from Metcalf which eluded him.

"No."

"No?" the voice asked in disgust. "Sullivan—"

"You heard me," Sullivan continued, unwilling to argue the point. The decision remained his and his alone. Riley's life was his to take, and he refused to do so without cause. "Agent Riley might prove useful."

Even if he was incorrect in his assessment of the situation there were other factors involved. Riley's death would bring Metcalf to bear, stronger and faster than he was prepared for.

Rallying the DSA behind the man's death would undo months of hard work separating them, dividing their loyalties into camps like sheep.

"I think you're wrong," the shooter said. Through the line the sound of metal dismantling resounded in his ear. "Especially if he finds out what you pulled here. Or my involvement."

"He won't," Sullivan said. "With Waters dead there is no reason to question anything further."

"You're welcome for that."

"I would offer my thanks, but I require more of you. I'd like you to take a more prominent role in what's to come."

Silence fell from the voice, the hard edge giving way to the blistering wind. Sharp static caused him to retreat from the phone. When the gravelly voice returned it was in little more than a whisper.

"What kind of role?"

"The DSA."

"A puppet," the man spat.

Sullivan grinned. The voice wasn't wrong in that assessment. Sullivan knew better than most, having steered the ship the last few months as deputy director.

"That is about to change."

"Your coup?" the voice scoffed. "You don't have the resources."

"Which is why we are having this conversation," Sullivan said. "*You* do."

"It won't be enough. Not for what you're considering."

Sullivan pressed close to his desk, looming over the console. Zac continued to work against the clock and a never-ending cipher of encrypted files. The one instrument required to guarantee Sullivan's rise to power was finally in the open thanks to the clumsiness of the Trust.

"I am working to secure our ascension as we speak."

"It will cost you."

Sullivan rolled his eyes. Everything cost. There was no avoiding it, and his check would be due sooner or later. "Name it."

"Riley."

Sullivan sighed. "When the time comes, you can have him."

"I damn well better for what he did to me."

"Of course." He leaned into the plush leather chair. Another ally had been obtained. He was another step closer to achieving his goal. "I will require a name to continue this relationship though. I know how you are about your anonymity."

"Until Riley is in the ground I only have one name," the voice snarled in his ear. "One name I want to hear him scream before I end his miserable life."

"Very well, then," Sullivan said, anticipation in his every word. "I will be in touch, Mr. Hendricks."

CHAPTER THIRTY-THREE

It was late the following night when Ben slipped out of the motel room. He had spent the morning recovering, the afternoon helping Morgan attempt to put her room back in order. By dusk, she was sleeping soundly, the physical demand of the day taking a toll with her injuries. Injuries he had inflicted upon her in his rage.

That thought had troubled him as he watched her breathing slow. He had hurt her, punished her for actions she'd never committed. Everything had seemed so clear to him in his anger, like a crystal ball revealing the truth behind all the lies. But the rage had been another lie, and it had cost him. There had been sadness in her eyes, and bruising along her skin. She forgave him and let it go completely as happenstance. Her focus was more on the rebel Clevinger's disappearance.

Forgiveness was more difficult from himself. His anger had almost ended her life. He wanted to stay close to her; he wanted to keep her safe and protect her as she healed. Unfortunately, Ben had other concerns. While he hated leaving and disobeying a direct order, he refused to depart his hometown without taking care of one last errand.

He traveled quietly through the city. At night there was a glow in the downtown sky; a dull hum resonated from the streets upward. A sweet aroma filled the snowy air, carrying memories of a past life in the city of his birth. A collection of feelings, thoughts, stories and events swirled around him as he walked. Each had molded the homesick agent into the man he had become.

Good and bad.

By the time he reached the small home on Breckenridge the city streets were deserted. The cold kept everyone bundled within their homes or firmly planted in the bar of their choice to escape the wintry mix blanketing the city with a fresh coating. It cleansed every corner with white.

The gate clanked loudly along the silent street as he entered the property. Each step crunched louder than the last until he reached the front porch and the crooked screen door to the home.

Emily Wright's home.

He had to see it for himself—to learn what happened. Ever since his calls had reached a dead end, Ben worried over her fate. The short, scrappy brunette had been his partner for years and a friend for even longer. Too much history lay between them for him to let it go. There was too much pain and joy tied to this place. He had to find out the truth—for her. He owed her that much.

The lock slipped loose, and the door swung open with a loud creak. Moonlight streamed through the scattered cloud cover. The lamp across the street joined the beams to illuminate the large oblong living room as he stepped inside.

Emily's parents had bought the home when they married. She had told the story to him dozens of times over the years. It was what they had spent their wedding money on instead of the fancy ceremony, the reception hall, invitations, thank-you cards, the disc jockey, and a dozen other items that were unnecessary to pronounce their love for one another. They had taken every dime they had, every scrap of savings they accumulated in their short lives, and found a place to grow. A place to cherish for the rest of their lives, instead of filling a photo album on a shelf in an apartment that never truly belonged to them.

After her mother had passed and her father had fallen ill, the home had gone to their only daughter. Emily treasured the gift. She had considered it a rite of passage. It was a family tradition she hoped to continue someday with her children. A piece of the city all their own.

That was what she told him.

Ben stood in the empty living room, which was devoid of furniture, boxes, everything but the growing cobwebs in the corners, and wondered what had happened to that dream—and the woman who preserved it. There had to be something. Some clue. Some indication of what had happened to his friend, his one true friend. Her past was here. She believed her future was as well, whatever that entailed. Emily had had a job she loved—people that loved her, friends that adored her. She had a life.

Now nothing but emptiness occupied the space.

From the desolate kitchen with cabinet doors still ajar, to vacant closets and bedrooms on the second floor of the small home, there was nothing left of her. Nothing but the memories they had shared together. Late-night beers after a shift from hell. Laughter shared. The first kiss that had changed everything for them.

Ben paused in the narrow hall before returning to the stairs. At the back of the home, the lone window in the space was boarded up by plywood. The dim light from the neighboring rooms allowed him to see small indentations in the plaster surrounding the shattered window. There were four along the right-hand side the size of his fingertips.

Bullet holes.

"What happened to you, Em?" he asked the darkness. Ben backed his way to the steps and shuffled to the first floor. His thoughts were distant, and his worries had finally been confirmed. Emily was in trouble and he had failed to keep her safe. He had failed all those he cared about, Morgan the latest in a long line.

Ben sat at the base of the creaky steps off the living room. His hands ran along his face as his imagination ran rampant with scenarios. He blamed himself. His ill-advised call for her help had put the target on her.

Now what? The question repeated through his thoughts on an endless loop. Finally, it was answered by a growing shadow on the wall at his side.

"It's been this way for the last six weeks."

Ben jumped to his feet, reaching for the sidearm he had failed to bring. He had been too worried about his state of mind to risk carrying a weapon. The drugs in his system clouded things, even after two days of recovery.

She stepped out of the shadows, tall and thin against the vast living room. The moonlight glimmered off her auburn hair and the pair of reading glasses peeking from her breast pocket.

"Metcalf."

"Before you ask, I only know that because of the call you made to her. When I looked into it I found the place this way."

Six weeks ago. She had known the entire time. Why was he surprised by that? "You could have told me."

"You also could have asked," she replied. "Instead of sneaking around behind my back."

"Don't play the wounded knight here."

"Don't play the petulant child," she snapped in return.

Neither wanted the fight. Metcalf wouldn't have come so far, journeyed into the field, simply for verbal sparring.

"Wait a second," he said, curiosity overcoming his exhaustion. "I ditched the surveillance. How did you learn about the call?"

"You never ditched *my* surveillance," Metcalf said with a smirk.

At the mall he had slipped away from the suits covering the food court. Only one other person had been near the restrooms. Ben shook his head. "The woman with the empty stroller?"

"Alison Adler. One of ours and a good asset." Metcalf nodded. "I figured she would be harder to pick up on while keeping track of Sullivan's goons."

"Sullivan?" Ben asked. The deputy director had put the blame squarely on Metcalf for the surveillance previously. *More games.* "Why?"

"You tell me," Metcalf said, moving closer. She kept close to the front windows of the home with constant glances to the vacant street. "He seems to have taken quite an interest in you."

"That's funny. He says the same thing about you." Ben answered, taking in the emptiness of the home in a new light. "Is that why Emily—?"

"I don't know, Ben," Metcalf said, her words soft. "I do think it has to do with your recruitment to the DSA."

"No," he muttered. He had spent so much time and effort keeping Emily out of the spotlight. During the trial, when she had wanted to take the stand in his defense. Afterward, at the courthouse when she had wanted to speak out to anyone who would listen—to save him from his fate. He had refused every attempt—to protect her. He had done it to keep her life and her career intact. Now they were as lost as his own. Even after everything, he was to blame. "Emily had nothing to do with what happened."

"No, but ask enough questions and someone is going to answer."

What questions were being asked? To whom? "Do you know...?"

"I don't." Metcalf's reply was barely a whisper. The lack of control over a situation was what Metcalf feared more than anything. "I wish I did."

"So you could keep it to yourself?"

"Ben—"

"Stop right there," Ben said, hand slapping the banister of the staircase. "You've been playing me from day one. For all I know you were behind Horace Waters and everything else."

Outside, the snow fluttered through the air in waves. Metcalf leaned hard against the window sill. The reflection of her blue eyes in the window stared through him. "In a way. Unfortunately."

Ben's heart stopped. "What did you just say?" Everything from his forty-eight-hour rage binge flooded through him. It started as a jumble, but he had slowly pieced together every interaction—including his time with Jamar Price.

"An older guy! Said you saw something you shouldn't have, something about that place on Wex and some dude you chased in there. He wanted to make sure you paid for it."

An older guy. "It was—"

"Sullivan," Metcalf confirmed, her voice emotionless. "Yes."

Ben rushed to her side, then pulled her away from the window. His fingers locked around her wrists and pressed her tight against the wall. The world went red. Anger swelled in his chest and his heart pumped faster. He blinked hard, sucking air in heavy gulps. Dropping her wrists forcefully, Ben fell back. He refused to give in to the remnants of the virus still in his system. "Tell me. Just tell me why."

"You found something he's been searching for in that house on Wex. Something he's been after for a long time. When you tracked his agent he had no choice but to clean up the mess. He paid Horace to handle things—to set you up. Sullivan paid a lot of other people to make sure it stuck."

"Horace," the name slipped from Ben's lips. The coincidence

of the man's death lingered. "Sullivan killed Horace. Or had him killed."

"Most likely," Metcalf said. "Once you were on your way here he saw the distinct possibility of you seeking out Mr. Waters for answers. He couldn't let that happen."

"Son of a bitch."

Metcalf reached for him. "If I had known I would have—"

"Don't," Ben fumed. He batted her approach away, then settled back to the steps.

Metcalf's hand fell to her side. "Fair enough. He's been playing us against each other, Ben. You have to see that."

"What was it?" The question gave her pause. Ben pressed harder. "What was in that house on Wex?"

"A weapon," Metcalf said. "An answer to a mystery I've been chasing ever since the DSA opened its doors. The ultimate tool."

"That's not an answer."

"It's called the Wellspring," she continued, pushing through his frustration. "I wish to God I knew more than that."

"Cut the crap, Metcalf."

"What do you mean?"

Ben shook his head. She was still holding back secrets, still kept some small truth from him. Her control over events came from those small truths.

"Fine. You don't want to talk about the Wellspring, then how about you level with me about my recruitment?"

"I don't—"

"The file, Metcalf. *My* file. Sullivan showed me the surveillance. Years before the trial and Horace. Years before the house on Wex. Before everything. Why?" She turned away from him. He refused to let the conversation stagnate, as the truth was long overdue. "Dammit, Metcalf. You ask for trust, for loyalty. Hell, you want me to lay my life on the line, yet you give me nothing. *Less* than nothing. You see that, don't you?"

"Ben…" She hesitated, working the words out. She was trying to spin it, when there was nothing left to spin.

"Forget it, Metcalf." Ben started for the door.

She stopped him when he reached for the handle. "Your father asked me to look after you."

"What? My… You knew him?"

Metcalf flashed a thin smile, stepping close to the confused and shocked agent. Delicate fingers pulled open his jacket. Her hand ran along the thin strip of material hanging from his neck: his father's tie. He had put it back on in the hotel room out of habit. It was a remembrance of the man who set him on his path.

"Whose blood do you think this is?"

From the job. Those were his father's words about the tie and the stains of blood coating the center. Where once his recruitment to the DSA and everything after the Horace Waters affair had occupied the top ten list of questions to be answered, now his entire life joined the competition. How could Metcalf know his father? He had only been a detective. He'd rarely ever left the city.

"How…?"

Metcalf let the tie fall against his shirt. The smile remained, distantly lost to memory. "I know you have questions. I wish I could stand here and answer them all. We're not afforded that time, unfortunately. He'll know I'm here by now, even with Stephanie stonewalling him. He'll know we're talking, and he's already making plans to counter it. Hell, there might be people en route right now."

"So talk."

"I need your help, but more importantly, I need your trust, Ben."

Ben shifted for the windows. He slid one open and the cold winter night rushed in like a flood. The chill soothed him, centered him. His eyes scanned the street. Suddenly, more shadows spread across the landscape, and the lamp post out front looked slightly dimmer than when he'd arrived.

"How?" Ben asked. Metcalf was a wall of secrets. How could he trust her? After everything he had read? After everything he had seen? "After Grissom…"

"Don't."

"Sullivan told me, Metcalf," Ben said. "About Grissom taking your job. About you sending him into Blake's lab on some bogus objective and risking his life to save your ass."

"The hell I did," Metcalf spat, fists clenched at her sides. "You can believe what you want about what happened to Jacob Grissom." Her eyes, calm and earnest, held a touch of sadness dotting the corners. The truth slipped through her defenses. "I miss him every day, Ben. I would never have let him go in that lab the way he did. I knew about the job. I wanted him to take my place. He deserved it. Do you understand?"

"Then who sent him in there, Metcalf? Who killed Grissom?"

"I don't know."

Ben nodded, looking back out the window. "Sullivan?"

"He's planning something," Metcalf said. "When it happens, everything we've worked for will be at risk. I won't let that happen. Can I count on you?"

He refused to meet her gaze. "I need time."

"I can keep you out of jail, Ben," she stated. "I know about the threats. I think it's time they stopped, don't you?"

"Stopping them is just another way to spin the sale, Metcalf. I won't be bought."

"I'm not trying to." She started for the corner of the room and the thin, black go-bag crumpled on the floor. Slipping her hand into the side compartment, she removed a small tin box. She held the offering out for Ben with both hands. "I understand this is a lot and that you need time. I know that. Time isn't on our side with this."

"What is this?"

"A peace offering." She stopped herself, nibbling at her lower lip. "It's the truth, Ben."

He sat on the steps of Emily Wright's empty home. He had come for answers and found only more questions. The director slipped the strap of the duffel over her shoulder, studying him closely though he refused to acknowledge her. His eyes were on the box which sat on his lap. He lifted the lid.

Inside was an old news article, a photo spread across the page—that of a young woman with auburn hair and blue eyes. Freckles dotted her cheeks. Beside her stood an older man in full dress uniform, the gold detective's shield gleaming from the camera flash. His father held a Susan Metcalf barely old enough to drive. The headline was in stark bold letters above the image.

COP SAVES SIX

Hero cop discovers child abduction ring.

She was telling the truth.

Beneath the article in the box were letters. There were dozens of them. Each one contained handwritten correspondence between a grateful child and her savior. Ben found more photos as well, including an old farmhouse in the country dotted by a white picket fence and those of another influential man in Metcalf's life: Jacob Grissom.

He held her differently than Ben's father had—closer and more tenderly.

Metcalf's head was low in the doorway. Ben let the photo of his father fall to the top of the pile, then he closed the box. Standing, Ben moved beside her. Tears dotted his eyes.

"Your father was proud of you, Ben," Metcalf whispered. "He might have kept that to himself, but it was there. He simply wanted more for you. For you to be more. To do more."

"That's not what *I* wanted."

She nodded. "He knew that too. We don't always get a choice in the matter though. Sometimes we have to carry a greater burden than we planned. Than we hoped. We have to. Or everything falls."

Ben cradled the box; he felt like a piece of him was inside, a hidden piece. It was the past he had tried to understand but never could.

"You should keep this," he said, extending it to her.

She took the small keepsake. "Thank you."

Ben leaned against the wall of the vacant home. Metcalf asked him to forget everything, to accept every experience with the DSA and lock it away as easily as she had. She expected him to put the past behind him and move for the future. He couldn't help but fear that future.

For months he had lived a life he never felt comfortable with. He had desperately tried to make sense of it all. People changed into trees. People lighting themselves on fire. Corrupt government agents. Ghosts. Everything bore down on him, and Susan Metcalf was asking him to understand it all. More than that, she needed him to accept the world she had brought him into.

In doing so, she made the same offer Sullivan had made previously. Who was right? Who was wrong?

Was there really any difference between the two of them?

"I need time, Susan," Ben said.

She nodded, tucking the box away, before she stepped out to the porch. She moved deeper into the growing darkness of the street until she melted into the shadows of the night. Her last words rang in his ears, as he continued to stand in the emptiness of his past.

"He's coming for the DSA, Ben. I am not going to give it to him without a fight."

ABOUT THE AUTHOR

Lou Paduano is the author of the Greystone series of urban fantasy adventures, which follow Detective Greg Loren and Soriya Greystone as they hunt myths, monsters, and legends in the city of Portents.

He is also the author of the conspiracy thriller series, The DSA, a serialized tale about a clandestine government agency trying to discover the true power behind humanity's future.

He lives in Grand Island, New York with his wife and three daughters. Sign up for his e-mail list for free content as well as updates on future releases at loupaduano.com.

THE GREYSTONE SAGA
AVAILABLE NOW

Follow the adventures of Soriya Greystone and Detective Greg Loren as they hunt dangerous myths and legends in the city of Portents.

**BOOK ONE - SIGNS OF PORTENTS
BOOK TWO - TALES FROM PORTENTS
BOOK THREE - THE MEDUSA COIN
BOOK FOUR - PATHWAYS IN THE DARK
BOOK FIVE - A CIRCLE OF SHADOWS**

ALSO AVAILABLE NOW

It's her first case and it might be her last.

Soriya has worked her entire life to become the Greystone — protector of her city, Portents, against the growing shadows of myth and legend. All her efforts are in jeopardy when she is struck down by the destructive power of the Minotaur.

Soriya must now find a new path. Only one thing is certain — she's going to need help.

The secrets of Soriya's training are revealed in the first adventure of this new Greystone trilogy.

THE DSA CONTINUES IN…

It is the DSA's darkest hour.

Branded as traitors, the field team lies in ruins. Ben Riley and Morgan Dunleavy are alone and on the run. Hunted on all sides, each must sacrifice everything to learn the truth about what's happened — not only to their own lives but to those they call friend and ally.

Old foes and familiar faces return to take advantage of the chaos — twisting the knife further with each betrayal.

In the midst of tragedy, answers come to light. The Wellspring stands revealed and nothing will be the same again.

Not everyone makes it out alive in this thrilling final chapter of the DSA's first season.